FIRE IN THE VALLEY

Spring is just around the corner in Llandyfan, and the first crocuses are beginning to bloom. Then the beautiful morning is shattered by the discovery of a corpse in the glebe — the victim of a grisly murder. Who could have wanted poor Fred Woolton, the mild-mannered milkman, dead? Midwife Maudie once again turns sleuth! Despite expecting a baby of her own, she is not about to take it easy while a case needs to be solved . . .

CATRIONA McCUAIG

FIRE IN THE VALLEY

A MIDWIFE MAUDIE MYSTERY

Complete and Unabridged

LINFORD
Leicester

First published in Great Britain

First Linford Edition
published 2016

A catalogue record for this book is available
from the British Library.

ISBN 978–1–4448–2879–5

Published by
F. A. Thorpe (Publishing)
Anstey, Leicestershire

Set by Words & Graphics Ltd.
Anstey, Leicestershire
Printed and bound in Great Britain by
T. J. International Ltd., Padstow, Cornwall

This book is printed on acid-free paper

Maudie Bryant gave a cry of delight when she noticed the first crocuses of the season, blooming bravely in the cold morning air. Three golden-yellow flowers and one purple one were fully open. Several more were still in bud, and she hoped they might be the purple-and-white-striped variety, her favourites. There was no doubt about it; spring was just around the corner.

This year, 1951, held definite promise for Maudie. The blooming of her garden bulbs was not the only thing bringing joy into her world. She was expecting her first child in late summer, and what could be more wonderful than that, especially for a woman who had long ago given up hope of becoming a mother? Less than a year ago, she had become the wife of Detective Sergeant Dick Bryant; and, some months later, had been shocked and thrilled to find herself pregnant at the age of forty-one! As a midwife, she knew that women's hormones were all over the place when they approached the menopause — sometimes causing increased fertility for a time, as if to offer a final chance at conception before they lapsed into middle age. Still, she hadn't dreamed that it could happen to her. Now that it had, it seemed like a miracle.

Perkin, the vicarage cat, sauntered around the corner and lowered himself down in the flowerbed, missing the crocuses by inches. 'If you scratch those flowers up, you'll be in real trouble, my lad!' Maudie warned. He ignored her and began to groom a hind leg.

She recalled with a sudden shock that she had left the larder window open that morning to give the place a good airing. Perkin had been known to get in there to see what he could find. She remembered the day he had polished off half a pound of butter — and then, as the final insult, regurgitated it all over the red tile floor. Muttering a curse, she flew indoors.

Nothing seemed to be missing except a

piece of cheese, and Dick might have had that. Her husband had a habit of looking into the larder at bedtime for some little delicacy to keep him going until morning. She could hardly blame him now that she was having odd cravings of her own, although Dick did not have the excuse of being pregnant!

She closed the window and stood back, wondering what they could have for tea that evening. There was probably enough leftover stew if she eked it out with a few dumplings; luckily, the pot had a heavy lid on it, which would have foiled the cat if indeed he had managed to weasel his way inside. Right, then! That was settled, so she might as well go out for a walk while the weather was nice. She decided to go down to the river and see if the pussy willows were out yet, but before she could put her plan into action, mayhem broke out in the garden.

She saw Perkin streaking past the window with a small brown dog in hot pursuit. Immediately afterwards, the sound of furious pounding on the front door set her heart racing. Taking a deep breath, she went to see what was happening.

She found an elderly man standing on the doorstep, looking agitated. He held a collecting tin in his left hand, using his right to steady the tray of small flags suspended from a cord around his neck. She had never seen the man before, but evidently the RSPCA was having a flag day.

'Just wait there a moment and I'll fetch my purse,' she told him, turning to go back to the kitchen.

'No, wait!' he replied, his voice quavering. 'Are you the midwife?'

Maudie frowned. 'Well, yes, I am, but I'm afraid I'm not working at the moment. If your wife or daughter needs help, you'll have to call Dr Dean at Midvale. I'll write the number down for you and you can give him a call. How far along in labour is she? You can call from here if it's urgent.'

'No, no, missus! I've come to you because there's a body. Under the hawthorn hedge. Up there in the glebe, it is.'

The glebe was open land belonging to St John's church. Church fetes and school field days were held there, and in between times the local people used it as a short cut to get from one side of the village to the other. Llandyfan, a community on the English side of the Welsh border, had long ago consisted of two hamlets, now more or less linked by scattered houses that had been built in Queen Victoria's time.

'Are you trying to tell me that you've discovered a body?' Maudie said, trying to make sense of this.

'Not me, missus, the dog did. Going crazy, he was, yelping and pawing the ground. I had to go and see what was upsetting him, and oh, I wish I never had!'

The dog in question had given up its pursuit of poor Perkin and was now at the man's side, looking pleased with himself.

'You'd better come inside and sit down,' Maudie said, ever the nurse. When Dick heard about this he would scold her for letting a strange man over the doorstep when she was alone in the house, but the poor chap was white and

5

shaking and she didn't want to be responsible for a second body if he collapsed. Besides, if he planned to rob the place, he would hardly have equipped himself with RSPCA collecting materials in order to catch her off-guard.

Her visitor followed her into the living-room and sank down on the chair she indicated. The dog arranged itself on the hearthrug, watching Maudie's every move.

'Now then, let's start again,' she said. 'I'm Nurse Bryant. You've found someone who may be injured, and you want me to come and see if there's anything I can do. Is that it?'

'Oh, there's nothing anyone can do for the poor devil, now, missus. Not when he's had his throat slit from ear to ear! No, I enquired at the shop, see, not knowing where else to find a telephone, and the postmistress told me to come to the midwife's house, on account of your hubby's a bobby, only not likely to be home at this time on a Monday morning.'

'I see,' Maudie said. As a nurse, she had seen plenty of dead bodies in her time, and more than one corpse during her years in Llandyfan. Even so, the thought of viewing some poor soul with his throat cut was repugnant to her now, especially in her condition.

'I'll call Midvale and report this,' she decided. 'I expect they'll send someone at once, probably my husband, and you'll have to wait until they get here because they'll want to speak to you, of course. I expect you could do with a nice strong cup of tea? I'll make you one as soon as I've phoned.'

★ ★ ★

'DS Bryant isn't in,' Maudie was told by the policewoman who answered the phone. 'I'll get in touch with Inspector Goodwood right away. You will hang on to that witness of yours, won't you, Mrs Bryant? Please don't let him get away. They'll want to speak to him.'

'Of course.' Maudie spoke stiffly. Did the woman think she was an idiot? It was on the tip of her tongue to inform her that she'd managed to solve several murders herself, thank you very much, but for Dick's sake she managed to swallow her indignation. He had only recently been promoted and she had no wish to cause trouble for him at work.

It seemed to Maudie that she sat at the table with her unexpected guest for a very long time before help finally arrived. Making small talk wasn't easy, and her natural inclination to learn more about the crime was tempered by the fact that she had no official standing here. If Dick's boss came to conduct the investigation, it wouldn't help if the man complained that he'd already told his story to Maudie and didn't see why he had to repeat it again!

Fortunately, it was Dick himself who finally arrived, accompanied by a screech of car wheels.

Maudie wrinkled her nose when he came rushing through the door. 'What on earth have you been up to, Dick Bryant? You smell like you've been burning rubbish on a bonfire!'

'Case of arson!' he whispered. 'Tell you later!' Looking puzzled at finding a dog on the hearthrug, he reached down to fondle the animal, who responded with a gurgle of pleasure.

'Now, then,' he began, when introductions had been made and a fresh pot of tea had been brought to the table. 'Let's start at the beginning. What were you doing in the glebe?'

'Collecting for the RSPCA,' the man said. 'I come over from Midvale on the bus, and I'm going from door to door, see? I did them streets all right, and then I thought I'd start over here. Only I didn't want to go the long way round by the crossroads, so when a lady pointed out how I could take a shortcut through that there field, that's what I did. I'm not so young as I used to be and that's a fact.'

'And your dog alerted you to the fact that something wasn't quite right,' Dick prompted.

'Oh, he's not my dog, sir! Never seen him before in my life. Come out of nowhere, he did. Making such a racket he was, I had to go and see. I don't know what I expected to find, but it wasn't that! Fair turned my stomach, it did. All that blood and gore! Thought at first the chap was wearing a red neckerchief, but . . . '

'All right, we get the picture!' Dick said, conscious of the pregnant Maudie beside him. 'I'll come with you now and you can show me where the body is. The police surgeon and the forensics team are on their way, and we don't want to keep them waiting. You can leave your bits and pieces here and pick them up later. They'll only get in the way now.' He turned to Maudie. 'I'll be back as soon as I can, love.'

'Oh, I'd better come,' she told him, lifting both hands up in a gesture of rebuttal before he could argue. 'I know everyone who lives in these parts, and your chaps don't. If I can identify the victim it will save you a lot of time and energy.'

'In your condition . . . ' Dick began.

'I've seen more dead bodies than you've had hot dinners, Dick Bryant! Just cover the poor man with something so I can only see his face, and I'll be quite all right.'

He heaved a sigh but made no further

protest. After locking up the house, the trio marched off down the street with the little brown dog trotting behind them. Once again, Maudie had found herself involved in a mysterious death practically on her own doorstep.

2

At the scene of the crime, the RSPCA man, John Landry, pointed wordlessly in the direction of an overgrown hawthorn hedge; under which Maudie could see what, from a distance, looked like a bundle of clothes.

'You two stay here,' Dick ordered, 'and keep your dog under control, sir, if you don't mind. We don't want the site tampered with any more than necessary.'

'He's not my dog,' the man protested again. 'Like I told your wife, he came out of nowhere. Just followed me when I was crossing the field.'

'Sit!' Maudie bawled, pleased when the dog obeyed at once. Somebody had taught him obedience, at least. She hid a smile when Landry sank down on the nearby stile. Surely he didn't think she was speaking to him? Perhaps it was just the proximity of the victim that had made him weak at the knees. Come to think of it, she didn't feel too grand herself.

'Good grief! It's Fred Woolton!' Dick cried. 'He can't have been here long. Didn't he call round this morning?' Fred was their milkman, an amiable fellow who had been known to Maudie for as long as she'd been in Llandyfan.

She took a step forward. 'Certainly he did. He came when you were in the bathroom, so I don't suppose you heard him. This was his day for settling up. Not that I talked to him at all; I just left the money in an empty milk bottle, same as I always do. He always comes — came — so early, and I don't like going to the door in my nightie. Poor Fred! Who would have done this to him? I'd have sworn he didn't have an enemy in the world.'

'And you were sure it was Fred who came, and not somebody else?'

She shrugged. 'Who else would it be? There's only one milkman in Llandyfan.'

'But you didn't actually see him?'

'No, I've said, haven't I? I waited until I heard the horse moving off and then I went to take the milk in. The money was gone and he'd left two pints on the step, same as usual.'

They stood in silence for a while, watched closely by the little brown dog. The sweet sound of birdsong came to Maudie's ears, followed almost at once by an altercation overhead as two small birds attempted to drive off a marauding crow. She was reminded of the war, so recently over, during which fighter pilots had valiantly fought against their enemies in the air. England was supposedly at peace now; yet even here, in their quiet country surroundings, death had intruded once more. Not for the first time, she asked herself what prompted people to kill each other in ordinary life. Wasn't it enough that millions had been wiped off the face of the earth during those six years of war?

Her unhappy reverie was interrupted by the arrival of several police vehicles screeching to a halt. Dick loped over to greet the newcomers, followed by the little dog. Maudie recognized one of the men as Dick's boss, Detective Inspector Bob Goodwood.

Landry seemed to come to life as the burly detective crossed the uneven ground towards him.

'Can't I go now?' he grumbled. 'I want to get home! If I miss the three o'clock bus there won't be another until six, and my bunions is giving me gyp!'

'Who is this?' Goodwood enquired, swinging around towards Dick.

'The man who reported finding the deceased, sir. Name of Landry, from Midvale.'

'Oh, yes? And what were you doing in Llandyfan, sir?'

'Collecting for the RSPCA, I was.'

'I don't see a collecting tin, sir.'

'That's at our house,' Maudie interrupted. 'Mr Landry came there to report the death and I asked him inside to wait until Dick got home.'

'Ah, Mrs Bryant,' Goodwood said, taking notice of Maudie for the first time. 'Someone will take your statement later.'

'But I've already told Dick everything,' she protested. 'Not that I know anything much, but . . . ' She caught sight of her husband's warning look and subsided.

15

Feeling annoyed, she watched his colleagues as they went about the business of erecting a screen around the body and stringing warning tapes around the murder site. There was nothing for her to do here, and suddenly she longed to be back in the secure place where she had been just a few hours ago, where spring flowers proclaimed the defeat of winter, and her own body carried the promise of new life.

'Please, I'd just like to go home,' she said plaintively, trying to sound more unwell than she actually was. Dick was at her side at once.

'That's all right with you, sir?' he asked Goodwood. 'She really shouldn't be out here like this, not in her condition.'

'I'm surprised that she's out here in the first place, Bryant, but yes, she might as well leave. Off you go, Mrs Bryant, and take Mr Landry along with you. I'm sure he can assist you if you feel a bit shaky on the road. We have your address, sir, should we wish to question you further, so please don't leave the country without informing us first.'

'Do you think they suspect me, Mrs Bryant?' Landry demanded, as they strolled back to Maudie's cottage. 'They always say that about not leaving the country, don't they? I've heard that in plays on the wireless.'

'Oh, that stuff's just fictitious,' Maudie assured him. She had always loved to listen to the adventures of Paul Temple. 'Besides, you didn't do it, did you? I mean, the guilty person must be covered in blood, and you look quite clean and tidy to me.'

She had meant that as a joke, but one look at his white face told her that she'd been taken seriously. She hastened to make amends. 'If they suspected you, I'm sure you wouldn't have been allowed to leave, Mr Landry. Now, here we are at my house. I'll just pop in to fetch your things and you can continue on your rounds until the bus comes.'

'Oh, I shan't carry on with that now,' he said. 'I'm much too shaken up. Would you mind if I came in for a little lie-down?

You can wake me up in time for me to catch my bus. Although I do think someone might have offered to drive me home! Twelve miles is nothing in one of those police cars. As it is, I'll take a cup of tea and have a bit of kip, and that should see me right.'

Maudie felt her pulse pounding in her ears. The nerve of the man! 'I'm afraid that won't be possible!' she said stiffly. 'And you've already had enough strong tea to sink a battleship. I'm sure you wouldn't sleep a wink after all that caffeine. A brisk walk in the fresh air will do you far more good, and there's a bench at the bus stop. You can rest there.'

Landry gave her such a black look that for a moment she felt quite frightened. Was he perhaps not as innocent as he made out? Having bumped off poor Fred, he might have come to report finding the body as a way to divert suspicion from himself. No, no! What about the absence of blood on his clothing? And surely whoever had committed the crime would be far away by now, eager to put as much distance as possible between himself and the glebe.

'Then I'll just come in and collect my things,' Landry told her.

'Oh, no you won't!' Maudie squeaked, aware that she sounded like a character in a Christmas pantomime. 'You stay right there and I'll fetch them out to you.'

She jerked her front door open and dashed inside to snatch up his tray and collecting things. She shot back outside, spilling a few of the little paper flags as she went. Relieved to find him still standing where she had left him, she thrust the items into his hands before stumbling back into the house. Banging the door shut hard enough that it rattled in its frame, she shot home the bolts, which were seldom used. They squealed in protest, and she made a mental note to get Dick to oil them before she was very much older.

'Thank goodness for that!' she muttered, sinking down into her favourite armchair, her heart beating far too fast.

'Aarf!' said a soft canine voice in answer. Somewhat bemused, she realized that the little brown dog was still with her, stretched out on the hearthrug as if it belonged there. She knew she should let him out so that he could find his way home, but suddenly she felt too weary to move. She hadn't behaved very kindly to poor old Landry; but, after all, she had no way of knowing if he was innocent or guilty of the killing, and anything might have happened if she'd let him come inside again. Surely he would understand why a woman on her own had to take precautions in a case like this, and forgive her for her seeming rudeness?

She asked herself why she was feeling so shaken. Did some primeval instinct warn her that Landry was dangerous, or were her hormones playing havoc with her good sense?

'Don't be such a fool!' she said aloud. 'You've just seen the murdered body of your milkman! Who wouldn't feel upset in those circumstances?'

'Aarf!' the dog said, wagging his stumpy tail.

3

'Poor old Fred!' Dick said, when he arrived home at last. 'Do you know, I don't think I've exchanged more than a dozen words with the chap in all the time I've been here. Is there anything you can tell me about his life outside of his work? Was he married, for instance?' Whereas Maudie had lived in Llandyfan for a number of years, Dick had only taken up residence there following their marriage the previous July.

'No, he never married,' she said. 'At least, not so far as I know. When I first came here, he lodged with an old shepherd, but he's passed on now. You know that cottage on the edge of the village that has purple clematis all over the front? That's Fred's home, or it was until this morning.'

'And what did he get up to when he wasn't working?'

Maudie shrugged. 'Fred liked his pint.

I suggest you talk to the old boys down at the Royal Oak. Apart from nursing him through bronchitis one winter, I didn't have much to do with him. As I said earlier, we mainly communicated by way of notes I put out with the milk bottles.'

'It doesn't give me much to go on,' Dick muttered. 'And why is that animal still here?' he asked, noticing the little brown dog for the first time. 'We'd better see him off. Somebody will be missing him, no doubt.'

'I think he's a stray,' Maudie replied. 'He's not wearing a collar and he's so thin. I gave him a plate of scraps just before you came in, and he wolfed them down as if he hadn't eaten for a week.' She smiled at the dog. 'Who's a lovely boy, then?' She laughed when he sat up and begged. 'We'll have to get you some bikkies if you're going to stay here, Rover!'

'Steady on, old girl!' Dick told her. 'He probably belongs to somebody. We can't just take him in off the street: that would be theft. Besides, I know I said I'd like a dog — and we've already decided to call it Rover — but I was thinking of a larger breed altogether. A collie, perhaps, or a Labrador retriever. This little character looks like a Heinz 57 Varieties!'

'I think he's a wire-haired fox terrier,' Maudie said.

'Oh, yes? As well as a few other things, I imagine. Look at that feathery tail!' As if he understood what they were talking about, the dog thumped his tail enthusiastically.

'So I shall make up a bed for him in the scullery,' Maudie went on, 'and tomorrow I'll put up a 'Found' notice in the window of Mrs Hatch's shop. If he hasn't been claimed in a week or so, I shall purchase a dog license, and Bob's your uncle!'

'In this case, Bob is my boss,' Dick reminded her. 'If that dog stays here, you'll have to be responsible for him. I shan't be spending much time at home in the near future, what with one thing and the other.'

'That reminds me. What were you doing before I summoned you this morning? You smelled like Guy Fawkes

Night and an autumn leaves bonfire all rolled into one.'

'Ah, now that's our latest nasty case — or it was, until somebody killed Fred Woolton. It seems there's an arsonist at work. Somebody torched the Baptist church at Midvale last night, and the fire wasn't discovered until it was too late to save it.'

'It's odd that nobody noticed a fire of that size.'

'Not really. The street it was on is at the edge of town, and there are no private houses nearby. Just the old shoe factory and a few small shops that were closed for the night.'

'But surely the fire would have lit up the sky? Someone should have noticed?'

'Not if the firebug did the deed in the small hours. It looks as if the fellow managed to break in and start the fire on the inside. It was a solid brick building, and it wouldn't have been all that easy to set the outside walls ablaze. That's only my thinking, mind. We have to wait for the official report from the fire brigade before we reach any conclusions.'

'Who on earth would be wicked enough to deliberately set fire to a church?' Maudie wondered, shaking her head. 'Perhaps it was youths, having a smoke.' But even as she said it, she knew it was unlikely. Even a carelessly dropped cigarette end could hardly set fire to a room full of pews or upright chairs.

Dick shrugged. 'Who knows what prompts people to do what they do? Anyway, I'm taken off that case now. Fred Woolton's murder has to take priority over here. I'll have to go from door to door trying to retrace Landry's route.'

'Is he a suspect, then?'

'We already know from the bus driver that he came from Midvale on the early bus. Therefore, Landry was in Llandyfan when the murder took place. We can't yet eliminate him as a possibility.'

'But he swears that he never saw Fred before he noticed the corpse.'

'Well, he would say that, wouldn't he?'

★ ★ ★

25

While Maudie prepared Dick's tea — baked beans on toast, with a poached egg on top — she found her mind working furiously. Poor old Fred had been such an inoffensive sort of chap. Who would want to kill him? He was hardly the sort to have had a secret liaison with someone else's wife — he'd been balding, inclined to fat, and fast approaching sixty. Rule out an irate husband, then.

Could he have been a secret gambler, perhaps? He might have racked up enormous debts he couldn't repay, and now some underworld figure had sent a hit man to teach him a lesson. No, that wouldn't do either. From what she knew from reading the *News of the World*, such thugs might have roughed him up a bit, even broken a bone or two — but not slit his throat. If they killed him, their money would be gone for good.

Perhaps Fred had simply been unlucky enough to be in the wrong place at the wrong time. In the course of his work — which involved going about the district early in the morning — he might have witnessed some crime, and been killed so he couldn't talk. Yet there hadn't been another death locally; not even a burglary. It was a mystery!

* * *

'Better not use all the milk,' Maudie warned, as Dick poured himself another cup of tea. 'Save some for your cereal in the morning. In fact, we'd better forget about having cocoa at bedtime. The weather's too warm for it anyway. I doubt they'll have found a replacement for Fred so soon. That's if they even know he's gone, poor man.'

'You'd better pop down to the shop first thing, love. Mrs Hatch keeps a few bottles on hand, doesn't she? Best get there early before the rush starts. I'm sure everyone else will have the same idea.'

Maudie nodded. The village shop was always a hotbed of gossip, and she might be able to pick up a few nuggets of information there. At the same time, she would put up a notice about the dog, hoping that he was indeed a stray and that nobody would come forward to claim him. She was already becoming fond of the little chap; and while she, too, admired the larger breeds that Dick fancied, there wasn't a great deal of room in the cottage and a big dog would constantly be underfoot.

'Come on, Rover!' He might as well get used to the name, she thought, as he followed her hopefully into the kitchen. She tried a few other names as an experiment. 'Ringo? Brownie? Fido? How about Sleuth? You did manage to detect a body!' The dog didn't move a muscle.

'All right, then, Rover it is!' she decided, passing him a toast crust. 'And there's no need to take my hand off at the elbow, my lad! We'll get you some proper food tomorrow, but until then you'll have to make do with leftovers. I don't suppose you fancy some rice pudding?' Apparently he did.

4

'Isn't it awful, Nurse?' Mrs Hatch's eyes were like saucers in her ruddy face. 'Poor Fred! It's a wicked tragedy, that's what it is!'

'Yes,' Maudie agreed. 'But then, it's a blessing that there's nobody left to mourn the poor chap.'

'Oh, but that's not true, Nurse! Didn't you know? He's been courting that Lillian Grant for years. You must know who I mean. She lives on Rosetta Street, the other side of the glebe.'

Maudie frowned. 'Lillian Grant? I don't think I know her, do I?'

'Happen not. She's sixty if she's a day, so you wouldn't have come across her doing your stuff as a midwife. She's a widow woman. Lost her husband in the Blitz when they were living in London. The way she tells it, their house took a direct hit. Her old man was asleep in the cupboard under the stairs, and didn't stand a chance. If it wasn't for the fact she was off doing her shift at the munitions factory, she'd have copped it too.'

'And Fred Woolton was courting this woman, you say? Who'd have thought it?'

Mrs Hatch scratched her neck, pulling a face at the same time. 'That's what they say, but who knows if it would ever have come to anything? What I do know is, he used to go there every Sunday and she'd give him his dinner. I don't know what she got out of it in return; perhaps he did a few odd jobs around the place, for all I know. Maybe she was lonely and liked a bit of company.'

'Every Sunday?' Maudie asked. Mrs Hatch nodded.

'Every Sunday for three or four years, regular as clockwork. I know that for a fact because he used to pop in here to pick up her Sunday papers. One time he bought her a little box of Cadbury's Milk Tray, said it was her birthday. She'll be missing all that now, poor soul.'

'But yesterday was Monday,' Maudie mused, following her own train of thought.

'And this is Tuesday,' Mrs Hatch agreed. 'So what?'

'Well, if your Mrs Grant lived over on Rosetta Street, Fred must have been taking a short cut across the glebe to get to her place. If Sunday was his regular day for visiting her, why was he there on a Monday?'

The postmistress shrugged. 'I don't see what's funny about that, Nurse! She probably wanted something doing and asked him to call. Monday's washday. Maybe her clothesline came down and she couldn't manage to fix it herself. She'd be up early to put the laundry in the copper, so she'd catch him when he came with the milk. He used to deliver over that side of the village, see? He wouldn't be able to mend the line then, or he'd be late with his deliveries and there'd be complaints, but she'd make him promise to go back after work.'

'But surely she'd have known on Sunday that her line was broken!' Maudie said. 'Why wouldn't he have fixed it then?'

'Oh, no, Nurse! A strict Methodist,

Fred was! He'd no more have done manual labour on the Lord's Day than stand on his head in the market square at Midvale!'

'Oh, well, I suppose Dick will get to the bottom of it sooner or later. I say, I don't suppose you know who this dog belongs to, do you?' Maudie indicated Rover, who was sitting innocently at her feet, panting rhythmically.

'I can't say that I do. Isn't he yours, then? I thought I heard you say your hubby was thinking of getting himself a dog, although I did think as you'd be storing up trouble for yourselves, with the baby coming and all.'

'We think he's a stray, Mrs Hatch, and if nobody comes forward to claim him I think we'll keep him. He's a nice little chap, so it seems a shame to send him to the pound and maybe have him put down.' Maudie thought it wise not to mention the dog's part in discovering poor Fred Woolton's murdered body, although — this being Llandyfan — the news was bound to get out in time.

'May I put this card in the window,

Mrs Hatch? If someone is missing him, I'd like to know as soon as possible. It wouldn't do to get too fond of him if he has to be returned.'

'That'll be sixpence, please, Nurse, and would there be anything else?'

'Milk!' Maudie remembered suddenly. 'That's what I came for, really. I'd better have two pints, please. No, make that three. I promised Dick a bread-and-butter pudding for his tea. And vanilla! I'd better take a small bottle of that. I'm almost out of it.'

'I got on to the dairy this morning,' Mrs Hatch said, twisting around to reach for the vanilla from the shelf behind her. 'Had to find out what's going to happen about deliveries now poor Fred's gone. It's not just the door-to-door deliveries, you know. I get my stock from the same place. They say they're interviewing a couple of chaps today and normal service will be resumed shortly. Fiddle-faddle! Sounds like one of them breakdowns when the wireless goes funny, eh? And what's it going to be like if they hire some fellow who doesn't know Llandyfan, you tell me that? He'll get himself lost! People want their milk delivered in time for breakfast, not halfway through the afternoon!'

'Oh, I shouldn't worry, Mrs Hatch. The horse will set him right. That animal could do the round on his own. He knows exactly where to stop and start. Why they want to hire another man at all, I don't know!'

'Ah, but could old Nobby collect the money, that's what I'd want to know!' Mrs Hatch said, laughing. 'If he tried to pick it up with those great yellow teeth of his, he might swallow a bob or two and get it stuck in his gizzard, and then where would we be?'

'Where indeed?' Maudie said. 'Come on, Rover, time to get back!'

★ ★ ★

Having put the milk away in the larder and offered the dog one of the newly purchased biscuits, Maudie felt too restless to settle to any housework. The weather was fine; why shouldn't she go for a nice little walk? It would do her good and the dog would enjoy it. She had meant to go looking for pussy willows on the river bank yesterday, before John Landry had come pounding on her door with his terrible news.

'Come on, Rover,' she said brightly. 'Walkies!' He jumped up, yelping, and began twirling madly. He knew that word. He must have a home and an attentive owner somewhere.

Maudie set off down the street, the dog at her side, but in some strange way her feet seemed to have taken control, for instead of heading for the river she found herself marching resolutely towards the glebe.

All was quiet when she arrived there. The warning tapes set up by the police were still in place, fluttering in the breeze, but she felt no compulsion to get any closer to the place where Fred Woolton's body had been found. It would be useless to go looking for clues. The forensics team had already been searching for evidence, and the flattened grass testified to that. It was only in novels by Agatha

Christie or Dorothy L. Sayers that useful clues were strewn about, such as match-books bearing the name of some city nightclub frequented by big-crime bosses! Even if such a thing *had* been left at the scene by the murderer, the police would have already discovered it. There was nothing left for Maudie to find.

Gazing into the distance, she could see the rooftops of the houses on Rosetta Street, half-hidden by the dozens of elms that nature had planted at the far edge of the glebe. Why shouldn't she go there and do a bit of snooping around? Dick might not have had time to canvass everyone as yet; and besides, she was armed with the new information about Fred's lady friend. She would have to share that with her husband anyhow, of course, but how much better if she could embellish it with even more useful scraps!

Even the most innocent of people were apt to withhold information when faced with a police investigation. Everyone had secrets; sometimes silly little things they felt ashamed of and would prefer to keep to themselves. Anything could come to light during an official investigation; useless for police purposes, but damning if the neighbours were made aware of the whole truth!

On the other hand, Maudie was a nurse! People trusted nurses and could often be relied upon to confide in a sympathetic woman. Yes, she would go ahead and see what she could find out, but what was the best way to go about it?

She stopped suddenly in the middle of the field. Rover came and sat at her side, looking up at her questioningly. 'I've got to go about this the right way,' she told him.

'Aarf!'

'I can't very well go from door to door, asking questions about this woman. It's not as if I have any official standing, and Dick certainly wouldn't approve of my getting involved in that way. No, I must go straight to this Lillian Grant. But what excuse do I give for poking my nose in?'

She could, of course, say that she'd come to offer her condolences for the milkman's death. Her friend Joan Blunt would have tackled it that way, but then she was the vicar's wife, and such things were expected of her. Maudie, however, had never met the woman — and what would she make of a stranger appearing on her doorstep, offering condolences out of the blue? Besides, there was only Mrs Hatch's word for it that Mrs Grant had actually had some sort of relationship with the murdered man. For all Maudie knew, she had offered him lunch as a one-off thing, and been stuck with having to entertain him on a regular basis when he'd misunderstood her intentions.

She looked down at Rover, who was obviously eager to get moving again. 'That's what I'll do!' she said. 'Why not kill two birds with one stone? I can go from door to door asking if anyone knows you, old boy. Off we go!'

5

'Coo-ee, I'm home!' Dick took a step backwards, almost knocked off-balance by the dog, who rushed at him, leaping up and trying to lick his face. 'Steady, old chap, you'll have me over!' Dick said, pushing the animal away to protect himself. 'Where's the missus, then?'

Maudie came slowly down the stairs, rubbing her eyes. He looked up at her in alarm.

'What's the matter with you? Is anything wrong?'

'Just been having a nap,' she told him, yawning widely as if to emphasize her point. 'We had a long walk today, and I may have overdone it a bit.'

'Oh. What's for tea?'

'Macaroni cheese and bread-and-butter pudding.' She had prepared these dishes before retiring to the bedroom, but as she said the words, she realized that it sounded like stodge. Her mother had always maintained that a heavy main dish should be followed by something lighter, like fruit jelly. People had been forced to ignore such culinary niceties when rationing was in force during the war and you were lucky to find anything edible, let alone part of a perfectly-balanced meal.

Luckily, Dick had no such qualms. Delighted to find two of his favourite dishes in the same meal, he trotted up to the bathroom to wash, leaving her to set the table. She wished she had some salad to go with the pasta, but it was too early in the year for that, unless you were willing and able to pay hothouse prices. She compromised by chopping up a bit of mustard and cress she'd grown on an old face flannel on the windowsill.

'So where did you go on your walk today?' Dick asked when he had polished off a second helping of bread-and-butter pudding. Pretending not to notice when he surreptitiously undid the top button on his trousers to accommodate his expanding waistline, Maudie tried to look nonchalant.

'I went round the village with Rover here, asking people if they knew who he belonged to.'

'And did you have any luck?'

'Not at all. Mind you, not everyone was at home at that time of day, so obviously I missed a few. Someone may see the notice I put up in Mrs Hatch's window, of course, but with any luck he's a stray and we'll be able to keep him.'

'Ah. Well, I'll be working on Rosetta Street and beyond tomorrow. I'll make enquiries about the dog while I'm over there.'

'Um, we went there today.'

Dick shot her an old-fashioned look. He knew his Maudie. 'Did you, indeed! And I don't suppose you just happened to mention poor old Fred Woolton while you were there, did you?'

She blushed. 'It could hardly be avoided! Everyone knows about the murder and there's nothing else on their minds!'

'Maudie Bryant! If I find that you've been asking questions and dabbling in matters that should better be left to the

41

police, I shall have something to say about it!'

'It isn't my fault that Lillian Grant's neighbour invited me in for a cup of tea!'

'And who the dickens is Lillian Grant, may I ask?'

'She was Fred Woolton's girlfriend,' Maudie told him smugly.

'Girlfriend? How old is she, for heaven's sake? I happen to know that Fred was sixty-two years of age. This one can hardly be a teenager.'

'Of course she isn't. It's just a figure of speech. She's a very respectable widow woman who Fred has been seeing for several years.'

'And she had hopes of him, had she?'

'It's more like he had hopes of her Sunday dinners. And there's no point you thinking she was hoping for marriage, and when he didn't come up to the mark she let him have it. Cutting a man's throat isn't a woman's crime, Dick.'

'And you'd know that, would you? Hell hath no fury like a woman scorned . . . '

'Actually, she wasn't a woman scorned. If you'll just stop interrupting, I'll tell you all about it. But before I do, you'd better take the dog out. Can't you see he's practically hopping from one paw to another over there?'

'Take him out? I've had a long and tiring day, Maudie. I'll just open the door and he can look after himself.' Dick heaved himself out of his chair and went to the door.

'No!' Maudie cried. 'If you don't go out with him, he may run off!'

'And wouldn't that solve our problem? He'd probably find his way home, if he has a home to go to.'

'Dick Bryant! You're the one who wanted a dog! And if we keep him we have to do right by him. We have to be responsible owners.'

'Owners, plural,' Dick muttered. 'Why should I be the one walking the wretched animal?'

Maudie smiled sweetly. 'Because you love me, and I'm pregnant with your child.'

Despite himself, Dick laughed. 'Oh, all right then! Come on, Rover! We men have to stick together!'

'Aarf!' said the dog.

Maudie had canvassed most of the houses on Rosetta Street before arriving at number nine. None of the housewives could throw any light on where Rover had come from, or who his owners might be, but they had all heard about the murder.

'He used to visit her at number nine,' one large woman with her hair in pink rollers said, her hazel eyes wide with excitement. 'Lillian Grant, her name is.'

'Oh, yes?'

'Lost her old man in the war, she did. Had to wait all these years to find another chap, and then this happens. It don't seem fair, do it?'

'They were going to be married, then?'

The woman scratched her armpit, breathing a sigh when this apparently relieved an itch. It reminded Maudie that she should check Rover for possible fleas, to nip any potential problem in the bud. He could have been on the road for days, sleeping goodness knew where.

'Well, I can't say as it had gone that far,' her informant murmured. 'Lillian Grant is one who keeps herself to herself, if you know what I mean. But we all like a bit of company, don't we? Now, if you don't mind, I'd best be getting on. I've got a cake in the oven, and by the smell of things it's almost done.'

Maudie thanked her and continued on to number nine, where she rapped on the door with growing excitement. The woman who opened it had a suitably lugubrious expression, and it seemed important to get to the point at once before she retreated inside again.

'Mrs Grant?'

'No, no. Don't you know me, Nurse?'

Maudie stared at the woman, racking her brains to put a name to the face.

'Er . . .'

'You delivered my grandsons, Nurse! Don't you remember? Two lovely boys. Four years old they are now, and bright as buttons. Course, I wasn't there for the big moment, or should I say moments? I arrived on the scene when you had them all cleaned up lovely.'

'Oh, of course!' Maudie remembered the babies and their courageous young mother, but she still had no memory of the granny, or what her name was. Fortunately, the woman was the chatty type, and she swept on with her tale.

'I live next door at number eleven, and I came round as soon as I heard about poor Fred, to see what I could do. I suppose you're here for the same reason, Nurse?'

'Well, I . . . '

'I'd ask you in, but I've just got her to lie down. She was wrung out, poor dear, and I could see she couldn't take much more, so I popped home and fetched a couple of pills that Dr Dean prescribed for my hubby when he couldn't sleep.'

Maudie bit back her usual little lecture about the dangers of taking medication prescribed for other people. She wanted to obtain as much information as possible to amaze Dick with; strictly in the interest of helping him with the investigation, of course!

'She was fond of him, then, your Mrs Grant?'

'Well, of course she was, with him being her only brother. Her only living relative, as far as I know. Naturally, she's devastated.'

6

'Her brother!' Dick said. 'Are you trying to tell me that nobody else in Llandyfan had any idea? Not even Ma Hatch? It's coming to something when the local gossips have missed that one! Why would this Mrs Grant let people think that Fred was her fancy man?'

'I don't think she 'let' them think anything of the sort, as you put it. According to the twins' grandma — and I still don't know her name — the poor woman was just desperate to protect her privacy. I suppose she had to confide in someone, and she trusted her next-door neighbour.'

'Who then blurted it all out to you!' Dick observed. 'With friends like that, who needs enemies?'

'And a good thing, too, if it helps you to solve the case. And you must admit that having a murder trumps any ordinary sense of loyalty when it comes to keeping little family secrets.'

Dick bit his lip. 'I shall have to call on your Mrs Grant first thing in the morning, or at least as soon as I can fetch a policewoman over here from Midvale to accompany me.'

'A policewoman! What's wrong with me, then?'

'Now, Maudie! This is murder, remember? This is an official investigation. You may like to think of yourself as the local Miss Marple, but there's no place for you in this.'

'And is your policewoman a nurse? Lillian Grant has been taking sleeping pills prescribed for somebody else, a practice I heartily disapprove of! What with that and the shock of losing her brother she's bound to be shaken up. What if she collapses during your little chat? You tell me that!'

'I'm sure that whoever I take will be well qualified in first aid, Maudie.'

'Piffle! That neighbour will vouch for me, I'm sure. Don't you think that Mrs Grant will feel happier with the local nurse in the room than some strange girl, still wet behind the ears? I tell you what! Why don't we let your boss have the final say? I'm sure you'll be calling him before you turn in, to bring him up to date on this latest development, so why not ask him if I can go along?'

Dick looked mutinous. 'Oh, yes? 'Please sir, can I take my wife along to hold my hand?' I don't think so, old girl!'

But the guardian angels who look after amateur sleuths were apparently on Maudie's side, for it was DI Goodman who suggested that she accompany Dick when he went to visit the victim's sister.

'The boss says you can come, if you stay in the background and keep quiet,' Dick told her.

'What? Are you sure? I bet he didn't put it like that, though, did he? What did he really say?'

'He said he can't spare anyone at the moment. There's been another fire, and it's all hands on deck. I've to carry on the investigation here, and as you happen to be a nurse, he'd be pleased if you'd be present during the interview with Mrs Grant.'

'Right-ho,' said Maudie, pleased. 'And where is this fire? Did he say?'

'Apparently it's the Wesleyan Methodist church at Brookfield. And before you ask, I can't say whether it's gone completely or if they managed to save it.'

'Do you think it's arson this time? Is it the same chap who did for Midvale Baptist?'

'The boss didn't say. I suppose we'll find out in due course. I say, is there any more of that bread and butter pudding? I'm feeling a bit peckish.'

'I was saving that for Rover's breakfast,' Maudie teased. 'You're a married man now. You have a wife who has to think of your waistline.'

'I could make you forget that,' he said, advancing towards her with a silly grin on his face. He was taken aback when the dog growled softly.

Maudie laughed. 'I think he's appointed himself as my protector,' she told him, bending down to smooth the dog's head.

'Protecting his pudding, more like,' Dick muttered. The moment passed.

The following morning saw them driving round to Rosetta Street, with Rover in the back seat of the official vehicle. 'On guard!' Maudie said, when the car came to a halt in front of number nine. Rover immediately moved into the driver's seat vacated by Dick, who rolled the window down partway to give the animal some air.

They had to wait for some minutes before the door was answered, and Dick was about to press his finger on the bell again when they heard shuffling footsteps approaching. Mrs Grant was an older lady with untidy white hair that made her resemble an unkempt poodle. She was clad in a grubby pink chenille dressing-gown and had fluffy green slippers on her feet.

'Good morning!' Dick said. 'I'm DS Bryant from Midvale CID. This is my wife, Nurse Bryant. May we come in?'

'I'm not sure I'm up to having visitors,' Mrs Grant said, rubbing a blue-veined hand over her face. 'I haven't been feeling very well. Could you come back some other time?'

'I'm afraid this can't wait,' Dick said. 'I'm investigating the death of Mr Woolton, and the longer we wait, the harder it will be to find his, er . . . attacker.'

'Oh, I suppose you'd better come in, then, but you'll have to excuse the state of the place. I'm afraid it's not very tidy. I haven't been able to do much since poor Freddie . . . ' She burst into tears.

Maudie put an arm around the sobbing woman and steered her back into the house. Dick followed, feeling inadequate. 'Shall we go into your sitting-room, Mrs Grant?' he enquired.

'We'll sit in the kitchen,' Maudie told him. 'I think a cup of tea is called for, don't you? I could do with one myself, Mrs Grant. Being in a delicate condition, I find myself craving a little pick-me-up at times, and tea always hits the spot.'

'I heard you were expecting, Nurse!' Mrs Grant said, fumbling in her pocket and bringing up a crumpled handkerchief. 'Fancy that, and at your age, too!

And I heard it's your first! How is it you never fell before?'

Maudie's cheeks turned a becoming shade of pink. 'We were only married last year, you see.'

'Oh, I knew that! Freddie used to tell me everything about the customers on his round. I just thought you might have been married before, and widowed, like me.'

'Oh, no. I never found the right man until Dick came along.'

'Like me and my Harry. One in a million, he was. I still miss him, you know. I hear something on the wireless, and I say to myself, 'I must tell Harry that,' and then I realize he's gone. Strange, isn't it?'

'Quite natural, when we lose someone we love,' Maudie murmured. 'And I'm sure it's the same with poor Fred.'

'I don't think I've quite taken it in yet, Nurse. It all seems like a bad dream. I keep hoping I'll wake up and find it isn't true.'

Dick groaned inwardly and went to the sink to fill the kettle. Here he was, a newly-minted detective sergeant, reduced to the rank of tea-boy while his wife and the person he had come to interview indulged in women's talk.

'He was your brother, wasn't he?' Maudie said softly.

Fat tears rolled down Mrs Grant's cheeks. 'I don't know how you found that out, Nurse! I suppose that Mrs Lemmon told you! I never should have trusted her, but it's too late now. Yes, Freddie was my brother. We were torn apart for so long, until the Salvation Army helped him to trace me a couple of years back. I was that happy, I can't tell you! Oh, why did this have to happen? It's not fair!'

'You were separated by the war?' Dick asked, finding his voice at last. She gazed at him for a long moment as if surprised to find a third person in the room.

'Yes, but not the war you mean, Mr Bryant. The war in South Africa.'

'The Boer War! That's a long time ago.'

'Sometimes it seems like yesterday. Dad was a soldier. He went off there leaving the four of us behind. Mum, me, and my brothers Godfrey and Fred. Well,

Dad was killed in battle at a place called Pretoria, and after that Mum seemed to go to pieces. Her pension didn't amount to much, and when she lost her job at the shirt factory that put the tin lid on it. She managed to find a job in service, but it meant living in and she couldn't take us with her. We had to go into the orphanage, Godfrey and Fred and me.'

'How old were you then?' Maudie asked gently.

'I was four. Fred was about eight and Godfrey must have been nine or ten. Mum told us it wouldn't be forever, just until she could save up enough money to take us home again. At least, sometimes I think I can remember her saying that, but perhaps I only know it because of what Fred told me.'

'Go on.'

'One day Godfrey wasn't there anymore. Fred was old enough to ask where he was and they said he'd gone to work on a farm, in a place called Canada. Ten years old he was, poor little boy. I don't know where he is today, even if he's still alive, but Fred promised he'd find him, if it took him all the rest of his days. And now he's gone, and I'm all alone! What am I going to do, Mrs Bryant? What am I going to do?'

7

Dick went out to the car to check on Rover. The dog greeted him with enthusiasm, leaping up to lick his face. This interview was getting him exactly nowhere! All it had achieved so far was to confirm that Lillian Grant was Fred Woolton's sister, which accounted for their Sunday get-togethers. Perhaps telling her story to Maudie would prove to be a good thing: at least she would have the relief of getting it off her chest. After that, she might be in a fit state to discuss the more recent happenings leading up to her brother's death.

Dick hardly knew what questions to ask. Could the roots of the murder lie in Fred's lifelong search for his missing siblings? Had he perhaps fallen afoul of someone from his orphanage days, who had gone to the bad?

'Come on, Rover,' he said, trying to clamp down on a sense of failure. 'We may as well stretch our legs and leave the missus to get on with it.'

★ ★ ★

Indoors, Lillian Grant continued her story with Maudie's encouragement. 'No, I never saw Mum again. The orphanage didn't allow visits from family members because they said it would unsettle the children. We weren't all orphans, you know. A lot of the children were like us, put there because their mothers couldn't provide for them.'

Maudie nodded. During her nursing career she had come across many people whose families had been scattered as a result of war. Lillian's story was by no means unique. 'I'm glad Fred found you in the end,' she said.

'Yes, after years of searching. We hoped to find Godfrey, too, and I always longed to know what happened to Mum in the end. I expect she died long ago, Nurse; she'd be well over eighty today if she'd survived. It's just that I'd like to know.'

'Of course you would,' Maudie said.

'And I shouldn't give up hope. After all, Fred found you, didn't he?'

'But now he's dead. Who would have done such a wicked thing, Nurse? My Fred never harmed a soul in his life. He didn't deserve to die like that!'

'My husband will find the person responsible,' Maudie said firmly. 'You can depend on that. And, by the sound of that doorbell, here he is now. I'll go to the door and let him in. Do you feel up to answering a few questions?' Mrs Grant nodded bravely.

★　★　★

'Mr Woolton was found in the glebe,' Dick began. 'Did he usually walk that way when he came to see you?'

'Oh, yes. It was the quickest way from his place to mine. Why would he come the long way round by the crossroads when he could just take the footpath from the church?'

'Quite. And he came to visit you as usual on Sunday?'

'Oh, yes. He never missed it. I always

gave him a nice roast and he enjoyed that. Not much good at cooking for himself. Beans on toast or a boiled egg was about his limit. Used to drink plenty of milk, though. He got that free, you see, on account of him working for the dairy.'

'And was that the last time you saw him?'

'Why, no. He delivered the milk as usual on Monday morning.'

'And perhaps you spoke to him then, and asked him to come back after work for some reason?'

Mrs Grant stared at Dick. 'I exchanged a few words with him, of course I did. It was his day for settling up, you see. Always collected the money Monday mornings, he did, for what I'd had the previous week. But no, I didn't ask him to come over later.'

'You say that Monday was collection day,' Dick went on. 'Could it have been a robbery gone wrong?' But even as he said it, he knew he was clutching at straws. Thanking her for agreeing to see him, he said that he would probably need to speak to her again, after which he and Maudie left the house.

* * *

By the end of the week Dick had discovered that, as was his habit, Fred had already deposited the money before taking his ill-fated afternoon walk across the glebe. An official at the Midvale Dairy had already explained the system to him.

'The milk goes over to Llandyfan on the local train via the branch line. It was Fred's job to be at the station when it arrived at five, to transfer the milk and cream to the float. He had a large round, but it was his proud boast that he could reach every one of his customers in time for them to have fresh milk for their early morning tea.'

'I know he came to us pretty early in the morning,' Dick agreed. 'My wife used to leave a note in a bottle if we wanted anything different from our usual pint.'

'Most folk did the same; Fred seldom had to knock on a door on collection day because they knew what they owed to the penny, and put the cash out on the step for him. A payment occasionally got missed, for one reason or another, but Fred kept good books and it usually worked out in the end.'

'And how did he deposit the money?'

'Ah, well, he used to send the empties on the train going the other way — that was our system — and on Mondays he hopped on the train himself, and came to us with the cash box.'

'And he did that on the day he died?'

'That's right, Sergeant.'

'I suppose you wouldn't happen to know where he went after that, Mr Bailey?'

The supervisor shook his head. 'No clue at all. He would have been on his own time then, you see. Mind you, if he died back at Llandyfan, he must have gone straight on the next bus, mustn't he?'

* * *

The following week, on speaking to the victim's sister again, Dick found that she had no quarrel with anything he had been told at the dairy. 'Did he normally come straight back after handing in the money, Mrs Grant?'

'I can't say as I rightly know, Mr Bryant. He didn't tell me all his comings and goings. I think he may have gone into the Spread Eagle now and then, just for a bite to eat, like. Teetotal was Fred, same as me. And like as not he went shopping over there if he fancied something for his tea that Mrs Hatch don't carry. Or say he needed to get new socks, or that. There's plenty of buses going between here and Midvale, so he could please himself as to when he came home, I suppose.'

Dick frowned. 'Well, let's say he came straight home last Monday. For reasons best known to himself, he decided to come and see you. Have you any idea what those reasons might be?'

'Do you think I haven't wondered about that? I've thought and thought, but I always draw a blank. What I find odd is that he was coming to me across the glebe. If it was that urgent for him to see me, it would have made more sense to get off the bus at the crossroads and cross over Jasper Drive to get to this street. Why go home first? That's what he must have done.'

'Perhaps he meant to go straight home, Mrs Grant. The first post would have come by then. Could he have received news he wanted to share with you?'

'He didn't do the football pools, if that's what you mean, Mr Bryant. Said it was a mug's game. So he couldn't have won anything he wanted to tell me about.'

'But you told my wife that Fred had been trying to trace your brother who went to Canada. Godfrey, was it? Perhaps he'd heard from the Salvation Army to say they'd tracked him down?'

'If only that were true! And yes, if it was something like that, he would have come to me right away, I know he would.'

★ ★ ★

Dick, going home to Maudie, still felt at a loss. A search of Fred's house might turn up a clue; although, if his suggestion was correct, surely the man would have taken the letter with him as proof of what the search had turned up. No such letter had been found on the body and, quite apart from what might have prompted Fred Woolton to cross the glebe in the middle of the day, they still had no idea as to what the motive for his killing could have been.

For Lillian Grant's sake, Dick hoped fervently that the answer wouldn't turn out to be one of those senseless killings when a pensioner was attacked and robbed of the few shillings he had in his pocket.

8

Maudie was waiting for the bus when her friend Joan Blunt caught up with her. 'Where are you off to, Nurse? Somewhere nice, I hope!'

Maudie pulled a face. 'I'm going to Midvale to see Dr Dean. No particular reason; just a routine check-up.'

'But you're a qualified midwife! I'd have thought you'd be able to check up on yourself!'

'Generally speaking, that's true, only now that I'm officially out of the workforce I don't possess a sphygmomanometer. I had to hand mine in.'

'What on earth is a sphgmo-whatsit?' the vicar's wife asked, looking so concerned that Maudie broke into a fit of giggles.

'It's only the gadget we use for taking blood pressure.'

'Oh, thank goodness. It sounds like a medieval instrument of torture.'

'No, no. Nothing like that. Are you heading for Midvale as well? We can sit together on the bus and have a natter on the way,' Maudie suggested.

'Yes, I want to go to Bentham's to see if they have any tea towels. I've had mine since before the war and they're only fit for the ragbag now. Would you believe it, this is the third time I've tried, but they haven't had a thing in stock.'

'Oh, no problem there! When I was in there last week I happened to notice a bale of tea towel material — red-and-white check, and just the right width. All you have to do is buy it by the yard and hem the ends. I managed to get three out of just two yards.'

'How marvellous!' Joan said. 'I'm so glad you told me. I'll go there straight from the bus depot and hope they haven't run out. Why don't we meet at Bentham's after your appointment? I'm sure you could do with something to keep your strength up before we head back.'

'Just what the doctor didn't order,' Maudie said with a wicked grin. The restaurant on Bentham's top floor was one of her favourite eating spots, and what was a trip to the big town without a treat or two to make life worthwhile? A chocolate éclair and a custard slice would go very well with a strong cup of tea. On the other hand, she mustn't put on more than twenty pounds during this much-wanted pregnancy, so perhaps she should stick to just one or the other. She sighed heavily.

'Something wrong?' Joan asked.

'Get thee behind me, Satan, that's all.'

Her friend nodded ruefully, under-standing the problem at once. 'I know what you mean! I had to let out that blue tweed skirt of mine again this winter, I'm afraid. It's all right for you, Nurse! Another few months and you'll be back to your original weight.'

'I wish!' Maudie groaned.

★ ★ ★

Dr Dean looked at Maudie over the top of his horn-rimmed spectacles. 'All seems to be well with you and Baby Bryant,' he told her. 'Have you given any thought to where you'll have your confinement when the time comes?'

'Well, at home I imagine,' she said, looking puzzled.

'You may be a midwife, Nurse, but I doubt you'd want to bring the child into the world without the help of somebody qualified to assist! And you know that Nurse Gregg isn't up to the job.'

Melanie Gregg was a young nurse who attended to the patients in the Llandyfan district, but she hadn't taken her midwifery training. Nor had she needed to, as long as Maudie had been on the job!

'I'd like you to book yourself into The Elms, Mrs Bryant.'

'The Elms, Doctor?'

'It's the new nursing home here in Midvale.'

Maudie had a vague recollection of hearing about this, but what with one thing and another she hadn't paid much attention at the time, it being outside her district. With her marriage to Dick, and now the expected baby, it had slipped her mind.

'I'd feel happier if you would consider it, Mrs Bryant. You must admit that forty-two is rather elderly for a first-time birth. Not that I'm expecting anything to go wrong, at this stage, but one never knows. And it's not as if you have a family member who could move in to give you a hand during your convalescence. You've told me that your mother is deceased, and you don't have sisters. Presumably your husband spends long hours away from home working at his job, and you can hardly expect him to get up in the wee small hours to attend to a crying baby.'

'I'll certainly give it some thought, Dr Dean. I'll discuss it with my husband and let you know.'

'Well, mind you don't leave it too long. The idea of this nursing home is catching on. The matron tells me they're already booked up months ahead.'

* * *

On her way to meet Joan at Bentham's, Maudie did indeed give the idea some thought. Giving birth in a nursing home held a certain appeal. In the event that something did go wrong — perish the thought — she would be much closer to the cottage hospital, where a caesarean section could be performed, giving the baby a better chance of survival. It would be lovely to spend nine days in bed, being waited on hand and foot, with other new mothers to chat to. And if she did stay at home, having to rely on Nurse Gregg's uncertain ministrations, she would probably find herself giving the girl instructions on what to do next. Not a happy thought when she needed to give all her mind and strength to deal with the birth process!

'I think it's a very good idea,' Mrs Blunt remarked, when they were seated in the crowded tearoom waiting for the waitress to bring their order. 'And since this Elms place is in Midvale, Dick will be able to pop in to see you now and then as his work permits. After the baby comes, that is. You won't want him hanging around while you're in labour.'

'Heavens, no!' Maudie said. 'I'm a bit worried about Rover, though. That is, if he's still with us by then. I'm beginning to realize that a dog is as much a responsibility as a child. We can't just leave him shut up in the house while we swan off for a week.'

'Your hubby could take him to work. Let him earn his keep as a sniffer dog or something. He found poor old Fred, didn't he? There you are, then! I'm sure I once read a novel where the detective took his boxer along with him.'

'Will that be all, ladies?' The waitress presented them with two fat little brown teapots and the necessary cups and saucers, teaspoons, sugar and milk. Maudie accepted her chocolate eclair, looking askance at her friend's choice.

'Are you sure that tiny piece of carrot cake is all you want, Mrs Blunt? We've got oodles of shopping to do before we catch the bus home. We must keep our strength up!'

'Carrot is a vegetable,' Mrs Blunt said virtuously. 'And what is more, I'm going to scrape this icing off and leave it on the side of my plate. So there!'

'Lent is over!' Maudie pointed out. 'We

don't have to suffer any more!'

'I bet you'd give your patients what for if you caught them eating eclairs in the middle of the morning! It would have been better for you and the baby if you'd chosen a nice raisin scone instead.'

'Spoilsport!' Maudie said, wiping a dab of cream off her chin with her paper napkin. 'Look, I've given up sugar in my tea, so it's a fair exchange!'

The two friends munched on companionably. Mrs Blunt absently scraped up the icing with her fork and devoured it with a little sigh of satisfaction.

'Here, I saw that!' Maudie said, laughing.

The expression on Mrs Blunt's face resembled that of her cat, Perkin, when he had managed to sneak some particularly tasty morsel. 'Summer is coming, Nurse! Think of all those salads and fresh fruit! The pounds are bound to roll off me then.'

Maudie left the store laden down with parcels. Each payday, Dick handed over what money he could spare, to be put towards purchasing the baby's layette.

The newly-decorated bedroom, now a nursery, already held piles of nappies, some made of muslin and others towelling.

'Surely we'll never need all those!' Dick had gasped, on seeing the pile that resembled the Leaning Tower of Pisa.

'A new baby can wet its nappy up to twenty times a day,' she informed him, 'and we need some to wash and some to wear, you know.'

On this day she left Bentham's with two tiny vests and six little flannelette gowns that fastened at the back with ties. 'Thank goodness clothes rationing is over at last!' she murmured, remembering how difficult it had been to find such items during the war, let alone manage to scrape together the coupons to buy them.

'Yes, we've finally managed to retire the parish layette!' Mrs Blunt said. This had been a small trunk filled with baby clothes that was loaned out to needy mothers.

''Needy mothers' covered just about everybody back in those days,' Maudie recalled. 'People were usually good about lending things to others if they didn't need the items themselves.'

'Most weren't so good at giving away the bigger items, as I recall! There was a time when you couldn't find a second-hand pram or a highchair for love nor money! I always thought it was so selfish for a woman to hang on to such things when she obviously had no further need for them.'

'Ah, you can put that down to superstition,' Maudie said. 'Women who hoped their family was complete were afraid to give that equipment away, because of the belief that as soon as they did so, they would fall pregnant again. And maybe 'superstition' is the wrong word for it because I've seen it happen, time after time.'

''More things in Heaven and Earth, Horatio . . .'' Mrs Blunt quoted, smiling.

9

'What's on the agenda for today, then?' Maudie asked Dick as he knotted his tie.

'Oh, more of the same. I want to make some enquiries in the Spread Eagle among the morning regulars. See if I can learn any more about Fred Woolton when he was away from home. I know he was a teetotaller, so it's likely that he frequented the pub just for companionship when he was over at Midvale. He may have let something slip while chatting to friends there.'

'Possibly.' Maudie was doubtful. 'I don't know how well you'd get to know people in the short time he must have been there, waiting for his bus home. You might do better at the Royal Oak here. Speak to Len Frost, why don't you?'

'And so I shall, but first things first. We must remember that something must have occurred on that Monday morning that sent Fred scurrying to see his sister.

He'd hardly have had time to stop in at the Royal Oak, so my best bet is the Spread Eagle. I've already spoken to the supervisor at the dairy, and there's no point in going back there.'

'You know best, Dick.'

'What are your plans for today, then?'

'I shan't be going far. To tell you the truth, I'm worn out after yesterday; enjoyable though it was, going through Bentham's with money to spend! Look what I bought!' She fumbled in a carrier bag and brought out several hanks of bouclé wool in a pleasing shade of fawn. 'I'm going to knit the baby a pram suit, only not in the first size. They grow so fast, and he or she won't need this until winter.' She held out a pattern book that depicted a helmet, a little coat and a set of leggings with feet attached.

'Very nice,' Dick murmured, planting a hasty kiss on her cheek before departing.

Men! She could have shown him a picture of a Zulu chieftain for all the notice he'd taken! Never mind. She could visualize the finished product, complete with a plump baby inside it. She wished she had a shilling for each of the times she'd seen a mother carrying a bare-legged baby whose upper half was warmly clad while the lower limbs were purple with cold. Maudie Bryant's baby would be wrapped up properly against the winter cold, or she'd demand to know the reason why!

'Cooee!' The back door swung open and Joan Blunt looked in. 'Don't get up! Can I come in? I'm not interrupting anything, am I?'

'No, no. I mean, yes, do come in, and no, you're not interrupting,' Maudie said. 'I'm just trying to summon up the energy to get on with my knitting.'

Joan walked inside, pulling the door to behind her. 'Oh, starting on that pram suit, are you? That knobbly wool you bought should be lovely to knit with. So many baby clothes are made with three-ply, and the garment may look beautiful but it takes forever to knit.'

'You don't have to explain that to me! That last matinee jacket I made was so fiddly I swore I'd never tackle a lacy pattern again. And it was the very devil to

79

sew together, matching up all the holey bits.'

Mrs Blunt nodded. 'Now, then, what I've come to tell you is that there's a special meeting of the Women's Institute today. It's called for two o'clock at the vicarage, if you feel like coming.'

'Oh, yes? What's that about?'

Mrs Blunt raised her eyes to the ceiling. 'Need you ask? It's about the Festival of Britain trip, of course!'

'Oh, that!' Maudie groaned. 'What's the trouble now, I wonder?'

Now that the war had been over for six years, the government wanted to underline the fact that the country was recovering. The Festival of Britain, to be held throughout 1951, was meant to show Britain's contributions to the fields of science and technology, architecture and the arts. Special events held in various cities, as well as travelling exhibitions, were all part of this.

Maudie had already sat through a meeting that had gone on and on as the women debated the pros and cons of their proposed bus trip. London, with its marvellous new buildings and exhibitions, was out of the question by virtue of the distance. 'And we don't want to go somewhere with a lot of walking involved,' one woman said firmly. As a nurse, Maudie had seen the state of the woman's bunions, and could sympathize.

Some liked the idea of going to Stratford-upon-Avon to see a Shakespeare play; someone else plumped for attending a concert of sacred music. Both suggestions had their detractors. Several of the women voted for an old favourite: a visit to a stately home where one could admire the antique furnishings, enjoy a cream tea, and on the way home stop somewhere for a fish-and-chip supper This was turned down as having no connection with the Festival year. The meeting had ended in acrimony with no decision having been made.

'Now the Mothers' Union are talking about setting up a rival trip, that's what!' Mrs Blunt muttered.

'That may be the answer,' Maudie mused. 'With Cora Beasley in charge, it'll be sorted out in no time.' Mrs Beasley owned the large estate near the village, and was the nearest thing Llandyfan possessed to a lady of the manor.

'Yes, but don't you see? If we have two trips, that will make things even worse.'

'I don't see how. Won't it give people a choice? Those who don't like choral music can see a play, and vice versa.'

'A lot of the women belong to both groups, or at least those who are Church of England do. I'm sure not many of them can afford to take part in both schemes, and that means they'll have trouble filling two buses! And that, in turn, will lead to bad feeling among the members!'

Mrs Blunt spoke in the weary tones of a vicar's wife who had endured years of having to pat down ruffled feathers among her husband's parishioners. If anyone had the mistaken idea that doing her job was easy, she could quickly disabuse them of the notion!

'I see it all now,' Maudie said. 'Some of them will want to throw the outings open to husbands and children, if only to make up the numbers. Then there will be people who don't want to go if there will be unruly youngsters on board, stuffing themselves with sweets and vomiting in the aisles.'

'Exactly!' her friend said.

'Well, then, I do believe I'll sit this one out,' Maudie said, grinning happily.

'Chicken!'

'No, honestly. There's no point in my taking part, because one way or another I certainly shan't be going on that outing. Too close to my time, you see. I'd be an utter fool to let myself get jiggled about on a long-distance coach. I've no wish to give birth somewhere in the wilds of Warwickshire!'

'No, of course you don't. That's that, then. You have the perfect excuse.' Mrs Blunt hauled herself to her feet. 'I suppose I'd better go and cut some sandwiches before the onslaught. All I've got to put in them is fish paste, but if there's a fight on perhaps they won't notice. That dog of yours is at the door; shall I let him out?'

'No, thanks. He's just hoping you're

going for a W-A-L-K, that's all. Don't encourage him.'

'Are you going to keep him, then?'

'I think so. He's a dear little chap really. If no one comes forward to claim him after this week, I'm going to get a license for him. Who's a boofuls boy, then?' she cooed at the dog, who padded to her side, staring up at her face in adoration.

'I suppose he's company for you when Dick is away.'

'Speaking of company,' Maudie said, 'you don't have to go for a minute, do you? There's something I've been meaning to ask.'

'Oh, yes?'

'It's about Lillian Grant, Woolton as was. She must be feeling so desperately lonely now, and as far as I know she's kept herself to herself ever since moving here. The only friend she's got seems to be Mrs Lemmon next door, and that has only come about since the tragedy. Perhaps you could invite Mrs Grant to go on the Festival outing, or maybe both of them?'

'Of course I can. Has she nobody else

in the world, Nurse? No children, or perhaps a sister?'

'She and Fred were brought up in an orphanage, you know. Their mother couldn't manage to keep them after her husband was killed in the Boer War, and for some reason she was never able to reclaim them.'

'How sad.'

'Fred managed to trace his sister after a great deal of searching, but they have an elder brother who has never been found. Apparently he was sent to Canada as a child on one of those work schemes for orphans. He may still be there, if he's still alive.'

'Dick Bryant!' Mrs Blunt cried, after a moment's thought.

'What?'

'Well, it's not that long since your hubby was over there on that police exchange, is it? And he did very well for himself, getting that medal and everything.'

Dick had broken an arm while saving the life of a toddler who had wandered into a field where a bull was grazing. He had managed to save himself from further harm from the huge animal by hurling himself over a fence, but he had landed heavily as a result.

'Well, then! They must think highly of Dick over there after that. Surely they have the resources to check for missing persons in Canada? Wouldn't it be wonderful if they could find this brother and put him in touch with poor Mrs Grant? What is the brother's name?'

'Godfrey, I think. Yes, that's it. Godfrey Woolton.'

'Thank goodness it isn't John Smith or Brown! At least it gives them something to go on, an unusual name like that,' Mrs Blunt said as she left the cottage.

10

The landlord of the Spread Eagle was a tall, burly man, with brown hair greying at the temples. Dick found him standing behind the bar with his sleeves rolled up to the elbows, polishing glasses with a blue-striped cloth.

'Sorry, sir. We're closed until eleven.'

'Police,' Dick told him, displaying his warrant card.

'Has somebody made a complaint? We keep strictly to the letter of the law here, sir.'

'I'm sure you do,' Dick said. 'I'm making enquiries about a man who may have called in here a week ago Monday, just before the bus left for Llandyfan and points north.'

'A week ago Monday!' the man repeated, turning around to lean on the counter. 'That's a bit of a tall order, isn't it? Unless it was one of our regulars, or the lunchtime crowd.'

'This would have been a chap wearing a long white canvas coat. In his sixties. Starting to go bald on top.'

'You don't mean that milkman that copped it up Llandyfan way? I read about that in the *Chronicle*.'

'I'm afraid so.'

'Well, blow me down with a feather! A chap like that quite often popped in here of a Monday, but I never caught his name. I thought maybe he worked for the dairy up the street.'

'And so he did, but his round happened to be at Llandyfan. The milk came over by train, but Fred Woolton — that was his name — used to make his collections on Monday and bring the money over to pay it in.'

'Ah. A robbery then, was it? Somebody who wanted to steal the takings.'

'No, it wasn't, because it happened in the wrong order. The victim paid the money in as usual and then he took the bus home. After arriving there, he set off again on foot, apparently to visit his sister who lives a mile or so away. Now, what I want to know is, did he stop in here while he waited for the bus?'

'Wait while I have a word with the wife. Her memory's better than mine. Vera!'

'What is it now? How am I supposed to get these ham rolls done if I keep getting interrupted?' A harassed-looking woman appeared in the doorway, frowning.

'This chap's a police detective, love. What did you say your name was?'

'Bryant. Detective Sergeant Dick Bryant,' Dick said, smiling in her direction.

'He's asking about that milkman what got himself murdered,' her husband said. 'Was he here on Monday? I don't recall.'

Vera rolled her eyes. 'He couldn't very well have been in here Monday, could he? Not if he was already dead like it says in the paper.'

'A week ago Monday,' Dick supplied. 'The day he was killed.'

'Oh, he was here all right, wasn't he, Brian? But he didn't stay. Don't you remember? When that other lot came in he looked like he'd been struck by lightning. He called out to that young chap, and what did that one do but bolt straight out again. Put his glass down on the table and rushed out the door after him, the one in the white coat did.'

Was this the break Dick had been hoping for? 'Can you recall what it was he said, Mrs Mackey?'

She shrugged. 'I couldn't be sure, not with all that racket from the jukebox. Something about hemming, or lemming, I don't know.'

'Let me get this straight,' Dick said. 'A group of people came into the pub; Fred seemed to recognize one of them, apparently someone he hadn't expected to find here; and he said something about lemmings, or lemons, perhaps? And the person he was addressing took fright and dived out again, with Fred hurrying after him. Is that about right?'

'I've said so, haven't I? Now, if you don't mind, I've got to get back to the kitchen. If I don't have food ready to serve when the lunchtime crowd comes in, my name will be mud!'

'But who were these people? Were they regulars?'

Brian Mackey scratched his head. 'Clerks from Barclays Bank round the corner, here on their lunch break, and a few from local offices — the estate agent's, the solicitor's and that. Maybe one or two of your lot. After they go back to work we get a few old pensioners in, retired men who come in for the company, making half of bitter and a bag of crisps do them until we turf them out at closing time. I'd soon go broke if I had to depend on them chaps for my living, but what can you do? Most of them don't have two pennies to rub together. I reckon I'm doing a public service, giving them somewhere to go,' he concluded virtuously.

'And I don't suppose you could identify this Lemon fellow?'

'Not a hope. Sorry!'

Dick thanked the landlord and went on his way. He would have to interview people at all the nearby locations in the hope of finding someone — or more than one person — who recalled seeing the little scene at the pub. Lemmon! Wasn't that the name of the neighbour Maudie had mentioned? A woman who had gone in to console Mrs Grant after Fred's death. But according to Vera Mackey it was a man that Fred had chased after. The neighbour's husband, possibly, or a son? And had he been bothering Mrs Grant in some way so that Fred had been determined to have a word with him? Neighbours fell out over all sorts of things: loud music played late at night, cats digging in other people's borders, branches hanging over into next-door's garden. Yes, that was definitely an avenue to pursue.

A return visit to the dairy turned up nothing of value. Visits to the various small businesses in the area were equally fruitless. Dick was beginning to wonder if everyone was operating on the principle of the three wise monkeys: see no evil, hear no evil, speak no evil. If only he could take people by the scruff of the neck and give them a good shaking to make them talk! Somebody must know something!

He had to leave the bank for another day. It closed at three o'clock and although the employees had to stay on for a while, to do whatever bankers did after hours, it would be difficult to keep them waiting while he interviewed them. It wasn't as if they'd witnessed the murder or been found at the scene of the crime.

If the truth be known, he was putting it off because he didn't fancy bumping into the bank manager, Arthur Ramsey. Some months earlier, Maudie had delivered the Ramseys' first child, a little girl named Peggy Ann. Her mother, Sheila, had fallen into a post-natal depression; which, Maudie told him, was not unusual and could usually be sorted out with treatment.

Ramsey was a brusque sort of man whose idea of helping was to insist that his wife snap out of it. After the poor woman temporarily abandoned her baby, a social worker had become involved, and there had been a danger of the baby being taken into care. It was Maudie who had contacted his mother-in-law, who gladly came to help out, much against Ramsey's will. When he continued to be difficult, Mrs Beadle had taken her daughter and grandchild back with her to Cornwall — where, by all accounts, the young mother was recovering well. What Ramsey thought of this was anybody's guess, but Dick didn't want his investigation hampered by personal feelings. Ramsey claimed to be on good terms with the Chief Constable, and Dick knew he had to walk a fine line between doing his job and getting a rocket from above. So he made up his mind to head for home, calling in at Mrs Grant's house on the way, and he'd tackle the bank in the morning when he was rested.

★   ★   ★

'Mrs Lemmon? No, Mr Bryant, she's a widow, just like me. And there isn't a son, just a daughter, a school teacher at Manchester, I think.' Mrs Grant seemed puzzled.

'The landlady at the pub did say it may have been 'hemming'.'

'That doesn't mean anything to me either. Could it be a person's name? Hemming?'

'Possibly. Where did Fred work before he came here?'

'Oh, he was at St Athan, that place in Wales where they flew those Hurricanes.'

'In the RAF, was he? Ground crew or something?'

'Oh, no, dear. He was too old to join up; they wouldn't have him. No, he was always a milkman. He got transferred to Wales to take the deliveries to the camp. I daresay they used a lot of milk, those poor young men. And in his spare time, he got a little job delivering all the vegetables and things they used there. It gave him something to do, I suppose, made him feel he was doing his bit. But what could that have to do with anything?'

'Nothing I can see at the moment,' Dick admitted, 'but I wonder if his death could have its roots in the recent past in some way.'

'We may never know,' Mrs Grant said, sighing.

11

Dick received a rapturous welcome from Rover. 'Where's the missus?' he asked. The dog looked towards the stairs. 'Up there, is she?'

'Aarf!' said Rover.

'It's a fat lot of good asking you anything,' Dick said, fondling the animal's ear. 'We'll have to teach you to speak English.' The dog rolled over, waving his paws in ecstasy.

'That dog will lap up all the attention you can dish out,' Maudie called from the kitchen. 'That and food! He's had two of the pork sausages I meant to give you for your tea.'

'You've never given that dog raw sausages, woman?' Dick was aghast at the thought.

'Not on purpose. I left them on the kitchen table while I went to answer the telephone, and when I came back two of them were missing. Bad dog!' Rover hung his head, looking so despondent that she had to laugh. 'That's all that my day amounted to. What about you? Are you getting anywhere with Fred's murder?'

'According to Vera Mackey — she's the wife of the landlord at the Spread Eagle — Fred was there on the day of his death, all right. He seems to have noticed a fellow he didn't expect to see there, and chased after him, shouting 'lemon' or 'hemming' or something.'

'That's the name of Mrs Grant's neighbour, Mrs Lemmon.'

'I recall your telling me that, but I've just been to see Mrs Grant and she can't see any connection. The woman is a widow with nobody other than a daughter in Manchester. I've spent the whole day going from one place of business to another without finding this chap, or indeed anyone else who witnessed the incident. Tomorrow I have to try Barclays Bank, and I'm not looking forward to that!'

'Oh, that's all sorted now,' Maudie said, instantly grasping what her husband

97

was thinking. 'Little Mrs Ramsey is back home now, under Dr Dean's care, and doing very well, I understand. I hope the man has learned something from their brief separation and is now treating her with more understanding.'

'And how would you know that, when she's not under your eye anymore?'

'Joan Blunt, of course. She's called in there once or twice, just so the girl knows she's not forgotten.'

'Good. So what are we having for tea: sausage and mash?'

'I'm afraid that would be more mash than sausage, thanks to that dog of yours,' Maudie told him. 'So I'm making toad-in-the-hole instead. Luckily I've a couple of eggs on hand for the Yorkshire pud.'

* * *

Some time later, when they were tucking into their meal, watched closely by the dog, Dick mentioned the case again. 'A lot will depend on what I learn at the bank, of course, but I may have to go away for a couple of days, down to St Athan.'

'Whatever for?'

'I'll have to discuss it with the boss, but I think the murder could have something to do with Fred's past. His sister mentioned that he spent the war years there — not in the air force, he was a bit long in the tooth for that, but he might have known the men at the camp.'

'The war has been over for six years, love. I doubt you'll find much there.'

'On the contrary, St Athan is still a viable operation. Young chaps get sent there to do their National Service. I seem to recall one of the coppers at Midvale mentioning that he has a son there. I know what you mean, though. Most of the fellows who were stationed there during the war will have been demobbed long since. Still, leave no stone unturned, as they say.'

★ ★ ★

The bank manager listened with growing impatience as Dick explained why he had come. 'I suppose I can't stop you speaking to my staff,' he said crossly, 'although I really must insist that our routine be disrupted as little as possible.'

Dick felt his temper rising, and strove to control it. He wanted to say that poor Fred Woolton's life had been disrupted, and finding justice for him was more important than keeping the bank's customers waiting for a few minutes. Thoughts of this officious little man complaining to Clive Marshall, the Chief Constable, made him count to ten.

'You won't need to speak to my tellers,' Ramsey said now. 'They're all women and you say you are looking for a man.'

'I'd like to speak to all your employees, sir, without exception. One of the ladies may have noticed something.'

Indeed, he hit the jackpot almost at once. 'I remember that!' one of the young women said. She was a curly-haired blonde with a bubbly personality. 'Some old boy in a white overall, like a milkman.' Her mouth opened in a wide grimace. 'Oh, no! Was he the one who got done in the other week? But what happened at the pub couldn't have had anything to do with the murder. That was Basil he was coming after, except that Basil took off running, like he didn't want to speak to the chap. I've no idea what all that was about. You'll have to ask him.'

'Basil?'

'Yeah, Basil Fleming, our Deputy Manager.'

'Thank you, Miss Rooney. You've been most helpful.'

★ ★ ★

'I'd like to see your Deputy Manager, please, Mr Ramsey,' Dick said, when he had spoken to everyone else and Fleming had not yet appeared.

'You'll have to stand in line,' Ramsey said grimly. 'He hasn't reported for work in more than a week, which is most remiss of him. He's not due any leave, and if he is ill then the bank requires a doctor's certificate from him. That has not been forthcoming.'

'Have you been to his flat, or his lodgings as the case may be?'

Ramsey glared at Dick. 'I am not the man's nursemaid, Bryant! He's old enough to behave responsibly, and if he cannot summon up the energy to let us know what the matter is, he will be replaced. There are plenty of men looking for work, you know, well-qualified men who have not been able to find suitable posts since returning from the war. The bank is no place for men who do not toe the line.'

'There is a murderer at large, Mr Ramsey. I suppose it hasn't occurred to you that Fleming might be lying dead behind closed doors somewhere?' Dick was glad to see that the bank manager's face had paled at the thought. Let him stew on that one for a while!

'This is a police matter,' Ramsey said, making a swift recovery. 'I shall find his home address for you, and you can continue your investigation from there!'

* * *

Dick learned that Basil Fleming had lived in a bedsitter in a large Victorian house near the market square. His landlady lived on the premises, and she greeted Dick with a mixture of fear and excitement in her expression.

'I've not seen him since a week ago Monday,' she said. 'Went off without a word to me to say he was going. Carrying a little grip in one hand and a briefcase in the other. Don't tell me you've brought bad news? Nothing's happened to him, has it?'

'Not as far as we know,' Dick assured her. 'We need him to assist us with our enquiries.'

Her eyes widened. 'That means you suspect him of something! What's he done, then, embezzled all the bank's money?'

'We don't know that he's done anything. He may have had to leave in a hurry to see to personal matters. An illness in the family, for instance.'

'Well, whatever it is, he'd better come back soon. He owes me two weeks' rent and I can't afford to lose that!'

'May I have a look at his room before I leave?'

'I suppose so. I don't usually let myself into my lodgers' rooms, but seeing as Mr Fleming seems to have disappeared, I suppose it won't matter, just this once.'

12

'And that got me precisely nowhere,' Dick told Maudie later that day. 'The rooms were just what you might expect. A bedroom with a washbasin in it — the lavatory is off the landing — and a tiny living-room-cum-kitchen. Well, the kitchen was more of an alcove with a hotplate and kettle. You know the sort of thing. There's accommodation like that all over Britain.'

'And you didn't find a single clue?'

'Not a one. The chap had obviously left in a hurry. The wardrobe door was wide open and there was nothing left in the drawers but the lining paper and a few mothballs.'

'No bloodstained clothing, then.'

'Nothing to link him with poor Fred's murder at all.'

'Then where were his clothes?'

'What do you mean?'

'He held an important position at the bank. He must have had to dress decently on the job. You'd think he'd have owned at least one good suit, and a few decent shirts, not to mention ties and socks. And what about off-duty stuff? Most men have a few pullovers and a pair of flannel bags, just like yourself. He couldn't carry all that in a small grip, surely?'

'You're right, of course. He may have come back to collect his stuff when the old girl wasn't in, or at night when she was out for the count.'

'And that's when he got rid of the bloodstained stuff,' Maudie said triumphantly.

Dick looked at her with his head on one side. 'This is not one of your favourite Agatha Christies, Maudie. Good police work is all about using scientific methods, not schoolgirl fantasies. Fred was killed here in the glebe, remember, not in some Midvale back street.'

'Oh, use your imagination, Dick Bryant!' his wife retorted. 'Just consider this. Your Basil Fleming has some dark secret in his past, something he was sure he'd managed to safely put behind him. He finds a new job in Midvale, and then one day a man who knows the truth — that's Fred — turns up unexpectedly and recognizes him.'

'Perhaps.'

'Yes, well, he can't afford to let his secret get out, so he runs. But he waits to see where Fred goes, which in this case is the bus station, and he follows him to Llandyfan where he kills him.'

'But Fred had already recognized this Fleming, remember. How does the chap get himself on the bus without being spotted?'

'You can't expect me to do your job for you!' Maudie said loftily. 'There could be half a dozen reasons. People queue up for buses, don't they? Fleming sees Fred in the line for our bus so he knows he's coming this way. Then Fred leaves for a minute — goes to buy a newspaper or to visit the lavatory — the bus arrives while he's gone, Fleming hops on and sits at the back, and Fred returns before the bus leaves.'

'I suppose it's possible, old girl, but that doesn't mean it's the way it happened. And even supposing you're right, and Fleming did kill Fred, how did he get away with it? If he'd caught the next bus back to Midvale with blood all over his clothes, somebody would have noticed.'

★ ★ ★

Dick reported Fleming's disappearance to DI Goodman, filling him in on the rest of his findings but carefully not mentioning Maudie's theory.

'Did this chap own a car?' Goodman demanded.

'I don't know, sir.'

'Then hadn't you better go and find out?'

'Will do,' Dick said. Mentally, he kicked himself for not having considered this before. Few ordinary people in the area owned cars: petrol had been strictly rationed during the war, and most people relied on public transport. Fleming had lived within walking distance of his job — why would he need to run a car? On the other hand, he probably made a fair salary as deputy manager, and he might have kept one for weekend jaunts to the country.

But a return visit to the bank earned him blank stares when he asked if anyone knew if Fleming owned a car. He would, of course, have to check through official channels, but meanwhile it looked as if Fleming could not have driven himself to Llandyfan; unless, of course, he kept a vehicle in some remote lock-up, unbeknown to his work mates.

★ ★ ★

Maudie, meanwhile, had taken Rover for a walk. And if their way lay across the glebe, who could argue with that? It was an area where the dog could run free, without fear of being knocked down by some speeding vehicle. And what more natural than to call in on Lillian Grant, to make kind enquiries about her health?

Hypocrite! said the little imp on Maudie's shoulder, but she dismissed the thought immediately. Yes, she meant to snoop, but her concern for the bereaved woman was genuine. And if a wife couldn't help to further her husband's career, of what use was she? Maudie rang the doorbell, feeling virtuous.

'Oh, it's you, Mrs Bryant! Do come in.' Lillian Grant seemed pleased to see her.

'I was just out walking the dog . . .'

'What a lovely little chap! I like dogs, although I don't have one myself. Do bring him inside.'

Rover trotted in, sniffing at the furniture with enthusiasm. Maudie watched him like a hawk, just in case he harboured any thoughts of lifting his leg against that horsehair-stuffed sofa, but he sank down at her feet with a happy sigh. She relaxed, wondered where to start. Luckily Lillian got in first.

'I've been racking my brains to think what it was that Fred might have said when he recognized that chap. 'Hemming' or 'lemming' or something, your hubby said.'

'Oh, he's got to the bottom of that, Mrs Grant. It was 'Fleming'.'

'Fleming? Are you sure?'

'Well, apparently it was a Basil Fleming who works at Barclays bank.'

'Fleming. Fleming. Now, why does that name ring a bell?'

Maudie sat very still, hardly daring to breathe.

'I don't know if it means anything,' Lillian said, biting her lip, 'but I do believe that Fred knew a Fleming chap when he was at St Athan during the war. Mind you, I can't say what his first name was. If Fred mentioned it, I've forgotten.'

'Can you tell me anything I can pass on to my husband? Anything at all? He's talking of going to St Athan to see what he can find out.'

'Oh, dear! I wish now I'd paid more attention, but when somebody is going on about people you don't know and things that happened in the past, you don't, do you? It grieves me to say it now, poor man, but Fred did ramble on a bit at times. I tried to look interested, but it wasn't exactly a glamorous career he had in the war, was it? Just delivering milk to an air force camp.'

'Go on,' Maudie prompted.

'Well, there was this girl. Linda, I think

her name was, or perhaps it was Lucy. Something starting with L, anyway. Fred had digs in the village, and this girl was his landlady's daughter. She was walking out with this Fleming at the time. You know what is was like in the war, Mrs Bryant. They built these great camps and brought in all these young men, and naturally that attracted all the local girls like wasps to a honeypot. The churches put on dances in the village hall — hops, they called them — and that was supposed to make the lads welcome, being lonely and far from home.'

As a midwife, Maudie had seen the unhappy results of some of those social events put on by well-meaning people. She thought she understood what Mrs Grant was driving at. 'He got the girl into trouble and then refused to marry her, was that it?' Although surely that could not explain what Fred had in mind when he came across Fleming again years later; or, for that matter, why Fleming should want to kill Fred to stop him from talking. It was a commonplace story, and even if Fred had been in love with the girl himself, he would have been forced to accept it at the time and get on with his life.

'Somehow I don't think that was it,' Lillian said. 'At least, she could have been in the family way as well, I suppose.'

'As well as what?'

'Well, him making off with all her savings, of course. They were going to be married as soon as they could afford it, you see, Fleming and this girl. According to Fred, she had quite a bit saved up in the post office, and this Fleming said he knew how to invest it so it would make a lot more interest. They'd have enough to put a down payment on a house after the war, and that would set them up nicely. He'd been in banking before he was called up, and he knew how to manage these things.'

'Ah, I see. And he made off with the money, did he, and was never heard from again?'

'I suppose that's what happened, although I really don't know any more than that, except that the RAF sent him away around that time. Posted, they call it. Makes him sound like a parcel, doesn't it?'

'This is all very interesting,' Maudie said. 'You won't mind if I pass this on to my husband?'

'That's quite all right, dear, although what good it will do us I don't know. Nothing is going to bring poor Fred back, is it?'

13

'And that's all she knows,' Maudie concluded when she had recounted her tale to Dick that evening. 'Shall you go down to St Athan now, and see what you can find out?'

'I might as well, if the boss okays it.'

'Then can I come with you?'

'Maudie, you know better than that. Besides, the boss may want to come with me.'

'Yes, but if he doesn't, why can't I come along? We could stay in a hotel in Cardiff and I could have a look around the big stores.'

'I don't think it would be wise to get jolted around in a train, not in your condition.'

'But surely you'll be driving if it's an official trip? Please, Dick! Don't leave me all alone here. Why not talk to Goodman about it? It won't hurt to ask. The worst he can do is say no.'

'What about Rover? The hotel may not take dogs.'

This gave her pause for thought. She had never owned a dog before, but she could see that having one did limit you when you wanted to be away. She realized for the first time just what having a baby would mean. You couldn't park a child in kennels as you would a pet. Her life was about to change in a very big way!

★ ★ ★

DI Goodman listened to what Dick had to say, gazing thoughtfully into the distance with his chin resting on the palm of his hand.

'Interesting,' he said at last, 'although I don't know if it gets us any further forward in finding this Fleming; or, for that matter, pinning the murder on him.'

'It might help to establish motive, sir. If Fred knew something to Fleming's discredit, a story the man wouldn't want to get out, he could have been killed to stop him talking. Stranger things have happened.'

116

'True enough. Well, I suppose it wouldn't hurt for you to go down to St Athan, see what you can sniff out there. Something might come in handy as background if Fleming ever comes to trial.'

Dick hesitated. 'I don't suppose you could send somebody else, could you, sir? I'd rather not leave my wife on her own at the moment, what with arsonists and murderers being on the loose.'

'*One* arsonist and *one* murderer, Bryant,' Goodman corrected. 'Still, this is mainly your case, and I certainly can't get away right now. I'll tell you what. Why don't you take a long weekend — you're due some time off after all the overtime you've put in lately — and take your wife down there for a little jaunt? Leave on Thursday, do your investigating on the Friday while she goes shopping or something, and spend time together over the weekend. Report back here first thing Monday morning with your findings.'

'I suppose I could . . .'

'Better take the chance while it's on

offer,' his boss said, grinning. 'You won't have time for little jaunts once the nipper arrives! Believe me, I'm an expert on these matters!'

'Yes, sir. Thank you very much. I'll speak to my wife and see what she says.'

★ ★ ★

Maudie, of course, was delighted. 'I knew you could do it if you really put your mind to it!' she said, flinging her arms round him and bestowing a smacking kiss on his cheek. Dick decided not to comment on his chief's role in making that decision. Why rob her of her illusions? Every man should be a hero to his own wife, at least once in a while!

'I'll just pop round to the vicarage to ask if they can take Rover while we're away,' she said.

'Right-ho, and I'll phone Cardiff while you're gone. Better not leave it too late and find we can't get a reservation.'

'Hadn't you better wait until we see what Mrs Blunt says? If Rover has to come with us, it might be better to try for a B&B. Most hotels tend to go thumbs-down on dogs.'

★ ★ ★

Joan Blunt agreed at once. 'I'll be glad to take the little chap,' She said. 'Who's a lovely boy, then?' Rover wagged his plumy tail.

'But what about Perkin? I'm afraid he isn't too well-behaved where cats are concerned.'

'Oh, don't worry about Perkin! He can go into the spare bedroom with a litter tray, and sulk there to his heart's content. That room has a nice wide windowsill where he can sit and watch the birds. There's a swallow's nest under the eave and he'll have the time of his life up there, grumbling and lashing his tail. Just as long as I keep the window closed, of course!

'And what about the vicar?' Maudie fretted. 'He won't mind, will he?'

'Far from it. I'll make him walk the dog, and that will help to relieve his anxieties a bit.'

'Mr Blunt is worried about something?'

'My dear, haven't you heard? That arsonist has struck again! At least, he tried to torch a chapel on the other side of Midvale, but fortunately some people turned up for choir practice and frightened him off.'

'Were they able to get a good look at him, I wonder?'

'Apparently not. Just a figure wearing dark clothing and a balaclava helmet. They didn't think much of it until they found the door broken open and a gasoline container on the floor inside. That's three churches or chapels now. Poor Harold is on tenterhooks in case the arsonist comes here. He was up at all hours last night, jumping at every little noise in case his beloved church was about to go up in flames.'

'Oh, well, Rover should be a help to him there. He's sure to be a bit jittery, staying somewhere new to him, so he's likely to bark his head off if anyone tries to break in.'

At that moment the vicar came in, and as if to prove her point Rover immediately let rip with a volley of sharp yelps. Maudie patted him and he stopped at once.

'Nurse is lending us her dog, dear,' Mrs Blunt said brightly. 'You see how he gives the alarm when someone comes in? That beastly firebug person won't come within a mile of the place with Rover on the alert!'

'That is very good of you, Nurse,' the vicar said, making Maudie feel guilty. 'I suppose you think I'm a bit silly, getting all worked up like this.'

'Not at all! It's a very worrying situation.'

'It is shocking to me that some misguided individual feels called upon to destroy the houses of God, Mrs Bryant. I suppose I shouldn't feel that we're a special case, here in Llandyfan,' Harold Blunt said. 'Those nonconformist chapels must be quite as dear to the hearts of their congregations as our church is to us, I know. But at the same time, they are modern buildings that can be replaced, although I'm certainly not minimizing the grief involved for their people if the worst happens, not to mention all the fundraising! But St John's is a beautiful stone church, built in Norman times! It's almost seven hundred years old! It can never be replaced, nor could the atmosphere within those walls. Think of all the people who have worshipped here down through the centuries. How they have brought their griefs to this hallowed place, to lay them at the feet of God.'

'I'm sure the police are doing their best to catch the culprit,' Maudie murmured. But what would happen when they did find him? It might be difficult to prove whether it was somebody with a mental illness, or a person who simply got satisfaction from destroying things. Was evil abroad in the world? No doubt Mr Blunt would think so. She hoped that their church would remain safe. Llandyfan wouldn't be the same without it.

* * *

'By the way,' Maudie said to Dick, when she returned home with Rover at her heels, 'Mrs Blunt had a good idea about something you can do to help Mrs Grant.'

'Oh yes?'

'She thought that your police friends in Canada might be able to trace her other brother, Godfrey. Wouldn't it be wonderful if they could be reunited? Even if he's dead, she'd at least know what had become of him. And perhaps he married out there and she has nephews and nieces, even his grandchildren! Think what that would mean to her, Dick!'

'It's a thought, all right.'

'Then will you write to your pals over there? Do it tonight and pop it in the post before we go to St Athan.'

'I'll do better than that! I've got the phone number of the chap I stayed with over there. I'll give him a ring right now. While I do it, why don't you go up and sort out what you want to pack for our trip?'

'That won't take long,' Maudie said gloomily. 'All I can get into nowadays are these wretched maternity smocks. I look like the side of a house!'

'And a very beautiful house it is, too,' Dick said, leaning over to kiss her.

14

Maudie and Dick registered at the Angel Hotel at Cardiff, and after enjoying a welcome cup of tea with buttered scones, they set out for a little walk. Cardiff's ancient castle was just around the corner, and they were delighted to find that the grounds were open to all. They sauntered along its pathways, admiring the massive flower borders that were ablaze with colour. Park benches could be seen along the route, most of them occupied by people enjoying the summer sun.

'I bet office workers come out here with their packed lunches,' Maudie said. 'That's what I'd do if I lived here. I wonder how old that castle is, Dick?'

'It was built in Norman times on the site of an old Roman fort,' he told her, having read a tourist pamphlet supplied by the hotel. 'I wish we could have a look round inside, but I don't think it's open to the public at the moment. We'll have to come here again when we've more time to spare. I'd like to have a look at the National Museum of Wales, for a start.'

'And I'd like to wander round all those arcades I've heard about, with so many fascinating little shops. I don't think I'm up to it just now, though!'

'Meanwhile, we've a job to do,' Dick said, as they headed for a convenient bench. 'At least, I have! You're just along for the ride, old girl!'

'No need to rub it in!' she told him. 'I'll behave myself. I'll be so quiet you won't even know I'm there. Just look at all that lobelia edging that bed of geraniums. Isn't it a heavenly blue? We could have some of that at home. I've been wanting to tidy up that border at the side of the cottage, but I couldn't decide what to put in it. Bedding plants would be the answer, don't you think?'

'Whatever you want, love.' Dick wasn't really listening. Maudie looked at him. She could almost see the wheels turning in his mind.

'Where will you start, Dick?'

'What's that?'

'When we get to St Athan. Do we go to the RAF camp?'

'I doubt that would help. As I said before, anyone who was stationed there during the war will probably have left long ago. No, as usual the pub seems the best place to start, and then the local vicar.'

'Then you mean to ask if anyone remembers Fleming?'

'Not necessarily. What would really help is if we can locate Fred's old landlady, the mother of the girl who was wronged by Fleming, according to Lillian Grant.'

'Wronged!' Maudie chortled. 'You sound like a country and western singer. 'He done her wrong.' Real sob stuff.'

'Never mind making fun of me, Maudie Bryant!' Dick retorted. 'Even you must be able to see that something must have been very wrong indeed if it led to murder.'

'That's if it really was Basil Fleming who dunnit,' she reminded him. 'We have no proof of that, do we?'

'That's why we've come here,' Dick

said. 'I'm trying to establish a motive for Fred's death.'

After a visit to the local pub, the Bryants experienced a surge of optimism. The landlord had introduced them to an elderly man by the name of Gwyn Rees, who remembered Fred quite clearly.

'We worked together at the Richards' market garden back in them days,' he told them. 'Leastways, I was on the production side, and Fred did deliveries. His day job was delivering for the dairy, but he moonlighted with us, said he wanted to get a bit put by.'

'You actually grew the vegetables then, did you?' Dick asked.

'Some of it. The rest got trucked in from other parts of Glamorganshire. The RAF camp was a godsend to old man Richards, otherwise he might have gone bust. Everybody with a bit of ground was digging up their roses and planting spuds and carrots instead. They wouldn't need to buy from us. Digging for Victory, that's what the government called it.'

'Yes, I remember,' Dick agreed.

'Of course, Dai Richards could have

sold what we raised anywhere, what with rationing on and food supplies being so short, but there would have been the cost of shipping, see? And if you priced things too high, people would accuse you of racketeering. You just couldn't win.'

'Would you happen to know where Fred stayed when he lived here?' Maudie asked. This trip down memory lane might be all very interesting to the old boy but it was getting them no closer to the reason why they'd come.

'Well, of course I know, missus. He had digs with Megan Jenkins up the road. She had a spare room, see, after her boy got called up for the army.'

'Is she still here, Mr Rees?'

'Oh, aye. Still living in the same place, that pebbledash house on top of the hill. She'll be that sorry to hear that Fred's gone. Murdered, you say? What's the world coming to, I ask you? Six years of war we've had, and the killing still going on.'

Mrs Jenkins was indeed sorry to hear the news, so much so that she burst into tears on the doorstep. Dick stood there feeling useless while she dabbed at her eyes with the corner of her apron. 'Well, I suppose you'd better come in,' she said at last, still sniffing miserably. 'Though I don't know what I can tell you. I haven't heard from Fred in years. Not since he left here after the war.' She peered at the car that was parked a few feet from her front door. 'Who's that you've got with you? A policewoman, is it, in case I faint?'

'No, that's my wife,' Dick explained. 'She's having a baby soon, and this is her last outing before the big day.'

'Well, you mustn't leave her sitting out there, boyo! Bring her inside and I'll make her a nice cup of tea! And I made a batch of Welsh cakes this morning. I must have known you were coming!'

Dick was partial to a nice Welsh cake, soft and flat and sprinkled with currants. He beckoned to Maudie, who immediately heaved her bulk out of the car and came to join them.

When the three of them were seated at the well-scrubbed kitchen table, with cups of steaming tea in front of them, Mrs Jenkins spoke up again. 'You haven't said how Mr Woolton was killed.'

'He was attacked, Mrs Jenkins. On his way to see his sister.'

Her eyes lit up at once. 'You mean he found his sister? Oh, I am pleased! I knew he was a Barnardo's boy, see. Had to leave her in the orphanage when they sent him out to work at the age of twelve. He never got over that, he didn't. Told me he wouldn't rest until he found her, not if it took him till his dying day.'

'He did find her in the end, and after her husband died, she came to Llandyfan to be near him,' Maudie said. 'But that wasn't quite what we wanted to talk to you about.'

'Oh?'

Dick thought it was time to step in. 'Do you know a man named Basil Fleming, Mrs Jenkins?'

The sudden change in her expression was alarming. Her face turned so pale as to give credence to the old expression 'white as a sheet', and her brown eyes glittered with distress.

'That rotten . . . ' she spluttered, apparently searching for a word that would express her feelings adequately without the need to resort to blasphemy.

Maudie picked up the teapot and refilled the woman's cup before stirring a heaping teaspoonful of sugar into it. 'Drink this, Mrs Jenkins. I can see you've had a shock.'

'Shock! If I can ever get my hands on that man, I'll give him 'shock'!' Mrs Jenkins swallowed her tea obediently. She seemed not to have noticed the liberty that Maudie had taken, and of course she had no idea that she was entertaining a nurse.

'Mrs Jenkins, I may as well tell you that Basil Fleming is our only suspect in Fred Woolton's murder,' Dick said, hoping that his questioning wouldn't lead to the poor woman's collapse. But Maudie gave him an encouraging nod, so he ploughed on. 'All we have to go on at present is that Mr Woolton apparently recognized Fleming, who has been working in Midvale. Fleming ran off and hasn't been seen since. There is a possibility that he killed Mr Woolton to prevent him coming out with something to his discredit. Now, if you can shed any light on what that might mean, it could be very helpful to our investigation.'

'I can certainly tell you all about that!' Mrs Jenkins said, squaring her shoulders and sitting up straighter on her wooden kitchen chair. 'I've waited a long time for that beastly man to get his comeuppance, and if he's committed murder as well, he deserves to be hanged!'

15

The ticking of the clock on the wall sounded unnaturally loud as Dick and Maudie waited for Megan Jenkins to begin her story. Finally, she heaved a sigh that was almost a sob, and the words came tumbling out.

'It all started when our minister told us we must provide a welcome for the young men who came here to St Athan,' she began.

'That was during the war?' Dick murmured.

'That's right. They came here from all over the place, you know. Not just England and Wales, mind, but from abroad, too. Places like Canada and Australia. Coming to the aid of the mother country, as one young chap said to me. Well, Mr Evans, who was our minister at that time, he said we should make them feel at home, for they'd given up everything to help us, and nobody knew if they'd live to see their own homes and families again.

'So that is what we tried to do. We had tea parties, and dances, and lantern slides in the church hall. Some folk gave card parties, but Mr Evans didn't approve of that. Work of the Devil, he used to say!' Mrs Jenkins laughed gently at the memory. 'None of us by here had much money to speak of to put on any grand events, but we shared what we had in other ways, and I think they were grateful.

'As time went on, some of the young men started courting local girls, and in the end there were quite a few war brides who went from here to places overseas, places we'd never heard of before. That was much later, of course. In the beginning they only went out together, doing the usual things, mostly taking long walks on a Saturday.'

All this sounded familiar to Maudie. It was a scenario that had been played out all over Britain during the war years.

'Well, our Linnie took up with this Basil Fleming. Elin is her name, but we always called her Linnie from the time she was a little thing. She brought him home to tea once or twice and we wondered if anything would come of it. Anything permanent, I mean. One thing we were grateful for, he was what they called ground crew. He worked at keeping the aircraft in trim, but he didn't have to fly them. I thought that at least her heart wouldn't get broken like some of them whose young men got shot down in flames. Oh, if only we could have seen into the future, it might have been a different story!'

'Did you like him, this Basil Fleming?' Dick asked.

'He seemed all right to me, I suppose. Clean and quiet. Not foul-mouthed like some of them. My husband got along well with him because they supported the same football team. That gave them something in common, you see. Yes, we thought he was all right, but the dog didn't take to him. That should have been a warning to me. Animals know, you see.'

'The dog didn't like him?' Maudie asked, thinking of Rover and wondering how he was getting along at the vicarage.

135

'No, he did not. He was a nice little dog usually, gentle as you please. Spot, we called him. Well, the very first time that Basil came here to the house, the dog met him at the door, growling and showing all his teeth. We calmed him down that time, but he still wasn't happy. Another time, Basil stepped on his tail — accidentally, I daresay — and instead of apologising and maybe giving the dog a pat, he kicked out at him. Cruel, that was. When poor Spot went for the chap and gave him a nip on the ankle, I didn't have the heart to scold him.'

By now Dick was moving restlessly on his hard chair. 'What happened next, Mrs Jenkins? What did Fleming do to upset your daughter?'

'They got engaged. I remember the night she came home to tell us about it. Like stars, her eyes were! 'I'm not having a ring, Mam,' she said, 'because we want to save for a place of our own. After the war, we'll have a nice little cottage and live happily ever after!'

'That was a joke, if ever there was one! Linnie had a little job at the fish shop, and everything she had left over after she paid us something for her keep at home, she put into her post office savings. Basil told us he was saving his pay as well. Then Linnie got left some money. I'd been in service as a girl, and I'd always kept in touch with my old mistress who was a very wealthy lady. She had no children of her own, and when she died she left a generous legacy to my daughter.

'This Basil, he'd been in banking before the war, and he said he knew how to invest her money so she'd get a better rate of interest. By pooling their money they could build up enough for a down payment on a house when the war was over. Give my hubby his due, he said it sounded like pie in the sky, but Linnie was head over heels in love and she trusted the chap. She gave him the money like he asked.'

'And I suppose she never saw it again,' Dick suggested.

'She did not, though it took a while before it dawned on her she'd been duped. Not long after that, he was posted, as they called it, and off he went to some place in England. I'm not sure now just where that was. Some place in Kent, perhaps, or Norfolk. At first he wrote to her once a week, and then the letters stopped coming.

' 'I hope he hasn't been killed,' she said to me one day, all upset and quivering.

' 'Of course he hasn't,' I told her. 'How could he be? He's not a pilot, is he?'

' 'No, but that place where he is could have been hit by enemy bombers, Mam.'

'That was the last we ever heard of Basil Fleming. I guessed he must have met some other girl there in England, and he didn't have the courage to come back and tell our Linnie. Or perhaps he really was dead. People do get knocked down by buses and that, don't they? My girl was broken-hearted, of course, but eventually she had to accept the fact that he probably wasn't coming back.'

'And the money, Mrs Jenkins?'

'Well, of course she wanted that back, didn't she? 'You'd better write to that place where Fleming put your money,' her dad said. 'It should have made a good bit of interest by now.' That got me worried because I thought, what if it's all in his name and we can't find him? How can Linnie prove that the money belongs to her?'

'And?'

'And it was worse than that; much worse. They wrote back and said there was no money and they'd never heard of any Basil Fleming. No such man had invested money with them.'

'You didn't take their word for that, I take it?' Dick asked.

'Na, na. My husband went up London and called on these people, just in case they were trying to pull the wool over our eyes. But it was a highly respectable firm of stockbrokers, whatever they are, and they told him that Linnie must be a victim of fraud, and there was nothing they could do. We reported it to the police, of course, but it came to nothing. Well, there was a war on, and there was more to worry about than one poor girl losing her life savings. A good many people lost more than that in the Blitz, see.'

139

Maudie had been listening with growing sympathy. 'Where is your daughter now, Mrs Jenkins? What became of her in the end?'

Mrs Jenkins got up and reached for a framed photograph on the Welsh dresser. 'This is Linnie. She's in New Zealand now. She went there with a family as nanny to their little boy. I was that sad to see her go, but perhaps it was all for the best. Making a new start, like. Perhaps she'll meet some decent chap out there and settle down.'

'Where does Fred Woolton come into all this, Mrs Jenkins?' Dick asked.

She blinked once or twice as if trying to recall who Fred was. 'He was staying here in the house all the while this was going on,' she said slowly. 'A sort of observer, you might say. He was sorry for her when it looked as if her chap had let her down, but we all know that these things happen in wartime, with people sent hither and yon. I remember him telling her, 'You're a lovely girl, Elin Jenkins. Someone worthy of you will come along one of these days, you see if he doesn't! Why, if I was a few years younger, I'd marry you myself!' She laughed at that. Fond of Fred, our Linnie was. She'll be that sick to know he's been killed.'

'And what did he have to say when it came out about the money?'

Mrs Jenkins held up both hands, palms outwards. 'He swore, that's what he did. Swore out loud, and he was a real gentleman most of the time, was Fred Woolton. 'I'll swing for that bounder if I ever catch up with him!' he said. And now the poor man is dead and gone. You never know what life has in store, do you?'

Perhaps Fred did catch up with Fleming, Maudie thought, even if it was by a strange coincidence. And that was why he had to die, to prevent him from speaking out. Fleming had a responsible job at Barclays Bank; he would lose that in a hurry if this story became known. Yet was that enough to commit murder for? Or was there an aspect to this story as yet undiscovered? Was it possible that Fleming had a history of fraudulent dealings, and this was only one small piece of the puzzle?

16

Maudie thoroughly enjoyed the rest of their weekend away from home. Although she didn't feel up to walking great distances, she did manage to wander through one or two of the winding little arcades, peering into the many little shops and wishing she had huge amounts of money to squander in them.

Dick, for his part, preferred the big covered market where not only vegetables, fruit and flowers appeared in profusion, but other useful or decorative items were displayed as well. Maudie, resting in their hotel room with her feet up, was touched when he came back from this expedition and presented her with a tiny bunch of purple violets. 'I almost brought you some golden mimosa,' he said, 'but it wouldn't have lasted the trip home tomorrow. These should be all right if you wrap them in a damp hankie.'

That evening they went to one of the

nearby cinemas to see *The African Queen*, one of the latest offerings from Hollywood. This was mainly because Maudie liked Humphrey Bogart, and although Dick wasn't keen on his co-star, Katharine Hepburn, he gave in out of deference to his pregnant wife. Cardiff, being the capital city, had its pick of the new films which usually took a long time to come round to their nearest cinema at Midvale.

'Did you enjoy it?' Maudie asked, her thoughts still with Bogart and Hepburn chugging along the Congo in an old boat during the First World War.

Dick pulled a face. 'I could take it or leave it, old girl. I thought it was going to be a jolly good war movie. Give me something with John Mills and Michael Wilding any day.'

'Never mind. You can choose the next time we go out.'

'Which may not be until we're old and grey,' he moaned in pretended despair. 'What would we do with the baby? It's not as if we could park a kiddie at the vicarage like we've done with Rover.'

143

'Oh, I don't know. Mrs Blunt might be delighted to babysit. I say, do you fancy something to eat? I don't know about you, but I'm feeling a bit peckish.'

'We could get sandwiches sent up to the room when we get back to the hotel.'

'I don't think so. I'd love a bag of fish and chips.'

'I don't know how we'd find a chip shop, old girl,' Dick said.

'And you call yourself a detective! When in doubt, ask!' On this summer evening, the wide streets of Cardiff were filled with people. Some, like the Bryants, had just left one or other of the cinemas, while others were simply out for a stroll, admiring the window displays in the big stores. Maudie sniffed the air like a Bisto kid. She spotted a large woman sauntering along with two small boys; all three of them carrying packages wrapped in newspaper. 'Excuse me,' she said, and moments later she darted down a side street with Dick in tow.

'What did I tell you? Perhaps I shouldn't have the fish at this time of night, but you can get me six-penn'orth

144

of chips, please, with plenty of vinegar and a pinch of salt.'

'Your wish is my command,' Dick told her.

* * *

Sunday found them heading home. While Dick kept driving at a steady fifty miles an hour on the side roads they'd chosen to follow, Maudie gave thought to how much she'd enjoyed their trip away, and said so to Dick.

'But what about you, love? Do you feel your visit to St Athan was worthwhile?'

'More to the point, will the boss think so?' Dick murmured, braking to avoid a fox that had darted across the road in front of them. 'All we really learned is that Fleming did in fact cheat Linnie Jenkins out of her savings by leading her to believe that he loved her, and planned to marry her. Reprehensible though that is, it doesn't make him a killer. Yes, Fred was fond of the girl, and wanted to catch up with Fleming and make him pay for what he'd done. Maybe he fancied himself in the role of superhero. He'd force Fleming to give back the money and Linnie would be eternally grateful. But, as I said before, does that really give Fleming a motive for murder?'

'It seems plain enough to me,' Maudie said. 'We know that Fleming has been working in Midvale. We know that Fred saw him in the Spread Eagle and recognized him. In turn, Fleming recognized Fred. Fleming runs, Fred follows. The next thing we know, Fred is dead and Fleming has disappeared. What more do you need?'

'Evidence,' said Dick. 'Proof, Maudie. What you say may well be true, but on its own, none of it will stand up in court. Now, if we could locate the murder weapon and find Fleming's fingerprints all over it, that would be a help! You can't hang a man on hearsay, old girl.'

Maudie subsided, feeling cross. She had promised to visit Lillian Grant after their return to Llandyfan, and she really didn't have anything hopeful to report.

'By the way, there's something I've been meaning to tell you,' she said suddenly, remembering that she soon needed to make a decision about the nursing home.

'What's that, then?'

'Well, you know I went to see Dr Dean the other day . . .'

Dick turned to look at her, alarm written all over his face.

'There's nothing wrong, is there? It's not the baby?'

'Oh, do keep your eyes on the road, man!' she squealed as the car swerved to avoid a large ginger cat. 'There really will be something to worry about if you land the lot of us in the ditch! No, there's nothing wrong. I just need to make up my mind about something. You know, I'd planned to have this baby at home, but the doctor thinks I might be wise to go into that new nursing home in Midvale. There's no reason to suppose that anything could go wrong, but I am getting on a bit to be having a first baby, and I'd get top-notch care in a place like that.'

'Sounds good to me, love. Why are you hesitating?'

'It's because I'm a midwife, Dick! Every baby born in the Llandyfan district in the past few years has been brought into the world by me! How will it look if I go in for something different for myself? It may look as if everybody else has had to make do with second-class care.'

'Maudie Bryant, that is absolute nonsense, and you know it! I may not know much about midwifery, but I know you've never lost a mother — and never lost a baby, either! Why, I remember how you delivered that little boy in the back of a car after his young parents slid off the road when they were planning to elope! Second-class care, indeed! If anyone dares to suggest such a thing, they'll have me to deal with!'

'Oh,' Maudie said, taken aback by his vehemence. But Dick hadn't finished. 'You just book yourself into the nursing home, old girl. I don't care how much it costs! You're very precious to me, and so is our baby! Nothing but the best for the pair of you!'

'Right,' said Maudie weakly.

17

Maudie went to inspect The Elms. She was still not quite convinced that she wanted to give birth there. A hospital was one thing, but a nursing home might not live up to those standards. If her baby was not to be born at home, then the surroundings had to be just right.

The Elms was a large Victorian house in Midvale, situated in a residential area. Most of the nearby houses had been converted into flats; nowadays nobody wanted private homes with so many bedrooms. The Elms, a huge barn of a place situated on the side of a hill, had formerly been a vicarage, attached to St Paul's church close by.

'I know they had large families in the olden days,' Dick said, looking up at the house in awe. 'Although surely vicars couldn't afford twelve or fourteen children, to warrant a barracks like this!'

'It wasn't a case of what one could

afford,' Maudie reminded him. 'It was a case of what you were sent. Even if they'd known much about birth control in those days, people probably thought it wasn't quite the thing. But I imagine they built these places to accommodate visiting clergy too. You know, when the Bishop turned up to deal with Confirmations, and so on.'

'I suppose so,' Dick said, kissing Maudie on the cheek. 'I must be off! You have a good time snooping around the nursing home, and I'll see you at home later. You're sure you'll be all right going back on the bus?'

'Of course I shall be all right! I'm not made of china, you know. I shan't break.'

Maudie climbed the steps to the front door and ran the bell. After a suitable wait it was opened by a middle-aged woman wearing a blue angora jumper and a tailored grey skirt.

'Can I help you?'

'I've come to inspect the premises,' Maudie told her. She received a frosty glare in return.

'If you are from the Department of

Health, we have received no notification of your impending visit. I'm afraid we are rather too busy at the moment. You'll need to make an appointment and come back another day.' She started to close the door.

Oh, dear, not a great start, Maudie thought. So much for making a little joke. Perhaps this wasn't going to be her sort of place after all. 'I am Mrs Bryant,' she said. 'Dr Dean has suggested I come here for my confinement, but perhaps . . . '

'Oh, I see!' the woman said, displaying a lot of very large teeth as she flashed a quick smile at Maudie. 'I'm so sorry, I thought you were someone else. Do come in, Mrs Byam.'

'Bryant. I'm Mrs Bryant.' Maudie stepped inside. 'Do I gather you've had a bit of trouble with the Health and Sanitation people?' (Because if you have, madam, I'm not sure I wish to come here! And if you can't even get my name right . . .)

'Not at all. It's just that we're all at sixes and sevens this morning. Matron

151

has had to go to a meeting of the governors, and I'm all on my own at the reception desk because my opposite number has gone to the dentist.'

'I see. Well, if I might just have a quick peep at the facilities, please, then I'll go and leave you to it.'

'Certainly. I'll be happy to show you around, but I'll have to dash back to answer the telephone if someone rings. It could be one of our expectant mothers in labour, you see, and it would be terrible if they were kept hanging about.'

'I quite understand,' Maudie told her. 'It's this way, is it? Up those stairs?'

Twittering, the receptionist led the way to the floor above. Maudie looked about her in approval when she was shown into a large, airy bedroom, with floral chintz curtains fluttering at the open window. The walls were painted a soothing pale blue, ornamented with a rather amateurish painting of an odd-shaped vase of blue hydrangeas.

'Lovely, that painting, isn't it?' the receptionist gushed, seeing Maudie's gaze on it. 'Matron does all our paintings herself. Everyone says she's quite gifted, you know!'

'Really' Maudie murmured. There wasn't much else she could say without appearing offensive.

The room was furnished in typical hospital style: two grey metal beds, bedside lockers in polished wood, over-bed tables on wheels that could be used to hold a tray of food, or for the patient to write letters on. Pretty floral bedspreads matched the curtains, and at the foot of each bed a neatly-folded pale green blanket promised extra warmth if the nights turned cool.

'Very nice,' Maudie said. 'Now I'd like to see the labour and delivery rooms, please.'

'Oh, I'm afraid I can't allow that, Mrs Botham. Not without Matron's say-so.'

'Why not? Are they in use at the moment? And by the way, the name is Bryant.'

'It's just not usual, that's all.'

'Just show me the way, please, and then I'll go away and leave you in peace.'

Maudie received another glare for her

pains, but having followed the woman downstairs ('If you don't mind, we won't take the lift; the sound of it wakes the babies'), she was soon peering at the labour room. This was much as she had expected; a two-bed room with another of Matron's daubs on the wall, this one depicting a jar of badly-executed shaggy chrysanthemums.

The actual delivery room met with her approval, like a hospital operating theatre in miniature, complete with a large overhead light which her guide switched off almost at once in case Maudie showed signs of stepping inside the holy of holies.

'I can't let you see the nurseries,' she said belligerently. 'We can't have people bringing in germs from outside, you know. But if there's anything else?'

'No, thank you. I've seen everything I came to see,' Maudie said, turning to leave. Presumably there were kitchens and bathrooms somewhere, and she hadn't met any of the nursing staff or the resident mothers, but those things did not concern her. 'Thank you for the tour, Miss Philpotts. I shall be making a booking in due course.'

The woman stared at her with myopic blue eyes. 'My name isn't Philpotts, it's Martindale.'

'Quite so,' Maudie told her, smiling sweetly. 'Goodbye, Miss Matthews. So pleased to have met you.'

★ ★ ★

'So what was your impression of The Elms?' Dick asked, when they were sitting down to their evening meal of cold ham, potato salad and sliced tomatoes. 'Do you think you'll go there?' He slipped a piece of ham fat under the table where Rover was waiting hopefully,

'Here, I saw that, Dick Bryant! How do you expect to teach that animal good manners if you indulge him at every turn?'

'Such a fuss over a tiny sliver of fat! Better it should go to the poor doggie than onto my waistline.' He patted his stomach as he said this. Sensing the movement, Rover stirred himself. He appeared at Dick's side with a pleading look in his warm brown eyes. *Can't you see I haven't been fed for a week, Master? Have pity on a poor dog!*

'Go and lie down!' Maudie said firmly. 'Go and chew on your bone or something.' Reluctantly, Rover left the table. 'Now, where were we?'

'I asked what you thought of that nursing home place,' Dick said.

'Oh, yes. Well, it's all right, I suppose. The place looks clean and comfortable, and well-equipped. I wasn't too impressed with the reception I got, though. The only person who seemed to be on duty there was a scatty woman called Martindale, who couldn't even get my name right. I suppose the nurses must have been out of sight somewhere, attending to their patients. That's if there *were* any patients on the premises at the time. I didn't hear any babies crying.'

'Oh, sure to be, old girl. Didn't Dean tell you the place is getting to be very popular?'

'Yes, but babies don't come to order, as I well know. You can go for days — weeks, even — without a baby in sight, and then they suddenly all come at once. A jolly good thunderstorm can have that effect, although doctors will always deny it. They say that's an old wives' tale, but midwives know better.'

'Then you will go there?'

'I suppose I might as well. I shan't have much to do with the receptionist woman, and the nursing staff are supposed to be well-qualified. And the bedrooms look comfortable enough, a cut above your average hospital ward. Although it's a bit of a lottery as to who I'll get for a roommate. At least in a hospital ward you have thirty or thirty-six women to choose from when it comes to finding someone nice to chat to. Still, it's only for nine days, and I understand there's a lounge somewhere on the premises where the mothers can congregate if they feel like it.'

'As long as all goes well with you and the baby, that's all that matters,' Dick said, suddenly feeling emotional. 'Don't mind me!' he sniffed, wiping a tear from his eye. 'A fine way for a hard-bitten policeman to carry on!'

Maudie looked at him with affection. Funny old Dick! She loved him to pieces, and she knew he felt the same about her. She was a lucky woman and no mistake. Then the doorbell rang, shattering the evening quiet.

She opened the door to find a uniformed boy on the step. He thrust a small envelope at her.

'Are you the nurse what's married to that detective? Mrs Grant on Rosetta Street said to bring you this on my way to Cubs.'

'Oh, thank you, dear. Just wait there for a minute and I'll see if I can find you a threepenny bit for your trouble.'

'No thanks, Missus. It's my good turn, see? We gotta promise to do one for somebody every day.' He sped off, leaving Maudie standing at the open door with a smile on her face.

18

'Here's a note from Lillian Grant,' Maudie said.

'For me, is it?' Dick asked, holding out his hand.

'No, it's addressed to me.'

'What is it, then? Women's Institute stuff?'

Maudie ripped open the envelope. 'Dear Mrs Bryant,' she read aloud. 'The police have finished with Fred's place and they say I can go there to dispose of his belongings. I don't fancy going alone and I wonder if you'd be kind enough to come with me? I promise there won't be any heavy lifting. It's mainly a case of deciding what belonged to him and setting it out on the doorstep for the Scouts to come and collect for their jumble sale. I shall be arriving at his cottage at about 2.30 on Thursday so if you could join me then I'd be very grateful. If you don't fancy it I shall

159

understand. There is no need to reply to this note. Yours faithfully, Lillian M. Grant, Mrs.

'Well,' said Maudie, 'I shall go, of course. I wouldn't mind having a look around Fred's place anyway.'

Dick looked stern. 'Now, Maudie, you're not to do anything stupid, do you hear me?'

She raised innocent wide eyes to his face. 'I don't know what you mean by that, Dick Bryant! Your lot have finished with the place, so I can't mess up any evidence. There won't be any heavy lifting, so I can't hurt the baby. I'll just be there as a bit of moral support for a bereaved woman. Where's the harm in that?'

'I don't know. I don't feel easy about it, that's all. Look, why don't you get Mrs Blunt to go along with you? Safety in numbers and all that.'

'Stop worrying. I'll take Rover with me. We'll be safe enough. I shan't sit down on any chair that looks rickety, and I won't drink the water or stand on a squeaky floorboard. All right, you old hen?'

Maudie was secretly pleased that Lillian had invited her to see Fred's cottage. Not that she expected to find anything of interest there; she was sure that the police had been very thorough. She just didn't like being left out of anything. She already knew that Fred had originally shared the rented accommodation with an old shepherd, who had since died. Presumably the few sticks of furniture belonged to whoever owned the place, and it was simply a question of Lillian sorting through any personal items to identify what might have belonged to her brother.

$\star \quad \star \quad \star$

Thursday came and Maudie set off with Rover trotting at her heels. The day was hot and she stopped by the wayside to pick a large burdock leaf to fan herself with. She waved it at the dog when he came sniffing around to see what she was doing. She had no wish to spend half the night removing burrs from his shaggy coat. In due course they arrived at the deserted cottage, the typical labourer's dwelling known as a two-up, two-down. Fred had been gone for a mere three weeks, yet weeds were already growing at the door and encroaching on the short path from the gate. She recognized dandelions and sorrel and shepherd's purse.

There was no sign of Lillian as yet, and Maudie lowered herself down on a large, flat rock that lay just inside the gate. She could only hope that she'd manage to lever herself upright again when the time came. Swallows were wheeling and darting overhead, and the air smelled of roses. With a sigh of pleasure, Maudie closed her eyes and dozed off. After a while, Rover gave a short, sharp bark and she came to with a start. She found Lillian Grant looking down at her, red-faced and perspiring.

'Oh, there you are, Mrs Bryant! I do hope I haven't kept you waiting long. I didn't mean to be late, but I had a bit of a fright coming across the glebe, and I had to turn back and come the long way round.'

'Oh, dear! What was it, loud youths pushing each other about or something?'

'No, I didn't actually see anyone. I just had a very strong feeling that I was being watched. Something seemed to tell me to run away, to get out of there as fast as my legs would carry me. Stupid of me, I suppose.'

'I've always believed that it's very wise to obey one's intuition,' Maudie told her. 'There is a great deal we don't yet know about the workings of the mind. On the other hand, I imagine that this is the first time you've walked across the glebe since Mr Woolton was killed?'

'Yes, yes, it is.'

'There you are, then. It's enough to give anyone the heebie-jeebies.'

'Of course, Nurse. You're quite right. Silly of me, wasn't it, not to think of that. And there was me fretting all the way here in case something nasty happened.'

'Not at all,' Maudie assured her. 'It's perfectly natural and only to be expected. Now, then, shall we go in? I may need you to help me to my feet. And speaking of feet, I'll be glad when I can see them again! I have to get my husband to clip my toenails for me because I can't reach them for myself!'

There was no sign of police occupation. 'I thought they'd have left a lot of white powder lying about,' Lillian said. 'You know, dusting for fingerprints and that.' The two women stood still and gazed around them.

The interior of the cottage was tidy, though sparsely-furnished. The main room, which had apparently served as both kitchen and dining room, held a wooden table, two upright chairs and an old-fashioned rocker, equipped with a worn cushion. A framed picture of King George V — not the present monarch, but his father — hung over the fireplace, and two small china dogs sat on the mantel.

'I can't say if those belonged to Fred, but the Scouts may as well have them,' Lillian said.

* * *

'If they belonged to old Ben, or whatever his name was, the chap can't have had any family, or at least nobody who thought to claim them, or they'd have been gone long since.'

'That warming pan is a bit of all right,' Maudie remarked, pointing to the said article hanging on the wall. 'It looks like real copper. If that goes into the sale, I wouldn't mind buying it myself. It's the sort of thing that gives a room a bit of class. I wonder who that belonged to? Maybe some relative of the owner of the house.'

'Well, now, I'll have a word with Vicar, see what he thinks about it. I want to have a look for Fred's papers. He told me he had a few National Savings certificates put away somewhere. He meant those to come to me if anything happened to him.' She fumbled in her skirt pocket for a lace-edged hankie, with which she proceeded to dab at her eyes.

Maudie, pretending she hadn't noticed, went to the bookshelf. 'Somebody liked reading Leslie Charteris,' she announced over her shoulder. 'There's three of his Saint books here. Good action tales! Dick loves those. And here's one by Ngaio

Marsh — *Death Invades the Meeting*. Oh, and a couple of early Agatha Christies! I see I'll have to go to that jumble sale!'

Rover, who had been enjoying himself sniffing around outside, suddenly began to growl.

'Is that someone coming?' Lillian asked, turning from the drawer in the kitchen table, which held an assortment of bits and pieces. 'I didn't invite anyone else to come along.'

'Turned up like a bad penny,' a male voice announced. A man stepped into the room, almost filling the narrow doorway. Not a big man, Maudie observed, taking in his rather dishevelled appearance, but there was an air of menace about him. Rover growled again. With a sick feeling in the pit of her stomach, she remembered Megan Jenkins saying something about dogs, and how they could spot a bad character.

'Who are you?' Lillian Grant demanded. 'What are you doing in my brother's house?'

He turned his head to look at her. 'Don't you know, woman? I'm an old friend of your dear departed brother, that's who I am.'

'You're Basil Fleming, aren't you!' Maudie gasped.

'Well, well, fancy you knowing my name! Never mind. Just give me what I've come for, and I'll be on my way and I shan't trouble you again.'

'There's nothing here that belongs to you!' Lillian said bravely.

'I want you to give me any papers that Woolton has left behind. Letters, notebooks, anything of that sort.'

'Then you'll have to wait because I've yet to come across anything of the sort. Just give me a forwarding address and go away. If I find anything that has to do with you, I'll send it on.'

'Oh, I doubt very much you'll do that,' he sneered, taking a step towards her, raising his fists. Lillian stumbled backwards in alarm, showing fear for the first time as the uncomfortable truth dawned on her.

'You leave her alone!' Maudie bawled. 'The police want a word with you, Mr Basil Fleming. They know you killed Fred

Woolton, and they'll be after you as soon as they find out that you've come back to Llandyfan!'

'That's quite unfortunate, because it means I shan't be able to let the pair of you leave here alive.' Fleming reached into his pocket and whipped out what looked to the terrified women to be an old-fashioned cut-throat razor. Under the circumstances, the commonly-used name was only too apt. Was this the weapon that had been used to kill poor Fred?

19

Dick! Where are you? Maudie's silent scream reverberated in her head, although she knew there was no chance of her beloved husband rushing to the rescue. The road outside Fred's cottage was deserted, and there was nobody to hear the two women if they shouted for help. Once before, she had been cornered by a murderer, and been saved at the very last minute by the arrival of a husband seeking her services as a midwife for his pregnant wife. No such help was forthcoming now.

A series of unhappy thoughts flashed through her mind in quick succession. She would never see her dear Dick again! They had been given such a short time together. Why must it be cut off now? And then there was her unborn child. She would fight to the death to protect it, but what chance did she have against a man armed with a razor? One quick slash across her throat would see the lifeblood gushing from her, and the baby would die with her.

As if he could read her mind, Fleming moved towards her, grabbing at her sleeve. Instantly Rover was on the spot, sinking his teeth into the man's trouser leg. Fleming kicked out brutally and the dog skimmed on his back across the flagstone floor, to end up cowering in a corner of the room, whining miserably.

'Now then, you can be first, Mrs Busybody,' Fleming snapped. He grasped her painfully by the hair as she twisted in his grasp, hoping to knee him in a vulnerable place, although she knew that this would only delay the inevitable.

Behind Fleming's back, Lillian Grant reached out and tore the copper warming pan from its place on the wall. The hook fell down and rolled across the floor. Raising the pan high as she tiptoed across, she then brought it down with all her strength on Fleming's head.

'Take that!' she shouted, looking at him with satisfaction as he crumpled to the ground.

Released from the killer's grasp, Maudie pulled herself together. She reached down and snatched up the razor, and headed for the door. 'Come on, do!' she yelled. 'Mrs Grant! Rover! Here, boy!'

'Where are we going?' Lillian panted, as they tore out of the gate and into the roadway.

'My place!' Maudie puffed. *Let somebody come! Let somebody come!* she prayed, but the road was deserted and there were no other dwellings nearby.

They made a pathetic sight as they hurried along with what speed they could manage. Maudie, heavily pregnant, was moving in a sort of hasty waddle. Grey-haired Lillian Grant tottered along in that peculiar way that women have when trying to run in high heeled shoes, rather as if their underwear is too tight. The dog brought up the rear, limping badly.

When they had gone about a hundred yards, Lillian faltered, clutching her side. 'Stitch!' she gasped.

'We must keep going!' Maudie muttered, her mouth dry. 'We've a mile to go yet. Oh, do come on!'

'What if I've killed him?' Lillian moaned, seemingly rooted to the spot.

'You'd better hope you have! What if he comes after us? He'll be desperate now and we shan't have a chance!'

'But what if I have? What will they do to me?'

'An eye for an eye, a tooth for a tooth,' Maudie quoted. Without waiting to see if the other woman was following, she set off again. Her first responsibility was to her baby. Rover seemed to sense the urgency and he surged ahead, occasionally wobbling along on three legs.

Maudie felt one of her shoes beginning to rub, but she tried to ignore the pain. She would have a fine blister there tomorrow — if indeed there was a tomorrow! If only they could reach home in safety, she was prepared to suffer almost any discomfort.

She wondered what Fleming was doing. She doubted very much if the blow from the warming pan had resulted in anything more serious than temporarily laying him out. Lillian was not a big woman, and even in the heat of the moment she surely could not have delivered a lethal blow. What would he do when he regained consciousness? If he had any sense, he would take himself off; but on the other hand, if his criminal doings were enough to merit his killing three people, would he take that way out? She doubted it. They must keep going until they reached the safety of her home.

'Let's stop at one of these houses,' Lillian gasped, as they passed a number of residences at last,.

'Might be nobody home,' Maudie puffed. 'No phones, anyway.'

When the church came in sight she longed to turn in at the vicarage, but the same warning applied. What if they found the Blunts absent and the house locked up, and Fleming caught up with them while they stood there dithering?

It seemed an age before they reached Maudie's cottage, and the three of them fell inside the front door, exhausted and thankful. Having put the door on the chain, she rushed through to the scullery to secure the bolts on the back door.

Lillian, meanwhile, went round checking that all the windows were firmly closed.

'Got to go upstairs,' Maudie muttered, heaving herself up one step at a time. She peered into her bedroom, then the nursery and the bathroom. Coming down again, she opened the door to the cupboard under the stairs, but there was nothing inside but her old Hoover, a jumble of cardboard boxes and an assortment of mops. She knew it was irrational — Fleming was outside somewhere — but she just needed to make sure they were alone in the house before she telephoned for help.

'Perhaps he's cut the wires,' Lillian quavered as Maudie removed the earpiece from her telephone, but fortunately all was well. Maudie was soon connected with the police station at Midvale, speaking to the officious policewoman she'd had dealings with before.

No, DS Bryant was not available, and neither was DI Goodman. They were out on a case. Would Mrs Bryant like to leave a message?'

'This is urgent!' Maudie huffed. 'You

must send men at once. Tell them that the suspect in the Fred Woolton murder is at Mr Woolton's cottage at Llandyfan. No, it can't wait until later. Don't you understand, woman? He is there now. He tried to kill us! What? What does it matter who else was there? Just send help, all right!' She hung up the phone.

'Honestly, I don't know why they keep that woman on! I know it was rude to hang up on her, but she should have been sending out reinforcements, not keeping me talking there.'

'She will tell somebody, though, won't she?' Lillian said anxiously.

'I should jolly well hope so, but just in case, I think we should be prepared. We don't have a gun here, unfortunately, so we'll have to make do with what we do have.' Maudie scurried about and assembled a carving knife, a toasting fork and a garden hoe. 'And if all else fails we can brain him with this,' she said, brandishing a galvanized bucket.

Lillian giggled nervously. 'After me letting him have it with that warming pan, do you really think he'd let us get close enough to get him with any of that lot?'

'He'll have to get up close and personal if he wants to finish us off. And don't forget that I brought his razor away with me, and I doubt he had two of them.'

'I don't know how you could bear to touch the horrid thing.'

'It's evidence,' Maudie reminded her.

Lillian's expression darkened. 'I hope I did kill him, even if they hang me for it! That monster killed my Fred, didn't he?'

'Yes, I'm afraid he did,' Maudie admitted. 'But no jury would sentence you to hang, Mrs Grant. Fleming would have killed both of us without thinking twice. I can testify that it was self-defence on your part.'

'They'll probably clap me in prison, though. I'll spend the rest of my days behind bars.'

'There is absolutely no point in thinking like that,' Maudie said, very much the nurse. 'You're in shock, Mrs Grant; we both are. What we need now is some good strong tea with plenty of sugar in it.'

'I don't take sugar, thank you.'

'You do now,' Maudie said, as she went to put on the kettle. Rover stirred in his bed and whined at her as she passed. 'Poor doggie,' she said, wishing she was able to bend down to give him a reassuring pat. 'Poor, brave doggie! I think we'll have to get the vet to take a look at you when all this is over. In the meantime, would a nice bikkie help you to feel better?'

'Aarf!' said Rover, thumping his tail. Maudie took the box from the shelf and dropped three into his basket.

'Oh, I wish they'd get here!' Lillian moaned. 'Why doesn't somebody come?'

'I wonder if I should phone police headquarters again?' Maudie muttered. 'Surely that woman has passed the message on?' An awful thought struck her. What if the policewoman had assumed that Maudie was hysterical for no good reason — a pregnant woman having a fit of the vapours — and had simply left a note on Dick's desk for him to phone home later? Perhaps Maudie hadn't expressed herself forcibly enough? It wouldn't hurt to call again.

The telephone was dead. Maudie jiggled the apparatus, to no avail. Quietly she replaced the earpiece on its hook.

'Changed your mind?' Lillian asked.

'Oh, I'd better not make a nuisance of myself. I'm sure somebody will be along soon,' Maudie said, attempting a smile. There was no point in getting Lillian any more upset than she already was. What would happen, would happen.

Now they were alone here: a pensioner, a heavily pregnant woman and an injured dog, with only a handful of household tools to hand by way of protection. And Basil Fleming must be lurking somewhere outside, with murder in his heart.

20

A heavy thump on the front door made both women jump. Rover barked loudly and came limping into the sitting room. The letter box rattled. 'Police!' came a loud male voice.

'Oh, thank the good Lord,' Lillian cried, jumping up to answer the door.

'No, wait!' Maudie shrieked, catching hold of Lillian's skirt to hold her back. 'It could be a trick! It may be Fleming out there!'

Lillian sank back in her chair, shivering uncontrollably. Lifting the flap, Maudie peered out through the letterbox, unable to see more than the lower half of a male figure, clad in navy-blue serge. 'Who are you? Who's there?' she demanded.

'Constable Todd Fry, Mrs Bryant.'

'Show me your warrant card, please!' Maudie had met Constable Fry before, but now she wasn't taking any chances. For all she knew, Fleming could be there too, holding a gun to the bobby's back and forcing him to cooperate. The requested identification came through the letterbox. Maudie relaxed and opened the door.

A large, cheerful young man stepped inside. Rover advanced, his tail wagging.

'Is everything all right here, Mrs Bryant?' Fry closed the door behind him.

'I think so, Constable. More or less! Where is my husband? Where is Fleming?'

'DS Bryant is at the late Mr Woolton's cottage. He sent me here to check that all is well. And is Mrs Grant here with you?'

'But Fleming! Where is he?' Lillian faltered. 'Is he dead?'

Fry frowned in her direction. 'What makes you think he's dead, Madam?'

'Because I . . . ' Lillian began, only to be shushed by Maudie. 'Hush up, Mrs Grant. Don't say anything until we can speak to Dick, or DI Goodman.' Lillian subsided.

'We received your message, Mrs Bryant,' the red-haired young man continued. 'DS Bryant and the boss are on the scene now,

180

but if Fleming was over there he seems to have scarpered.'

'He certainly was there!' Maudie snapped. 'He tried to kill us! If you don't believe me, just look at my poor dog! That brute of a man kicked him across the room when he tried to protect me!'

'Somebody in authority will be along shortly, and you can tell your story then,' Fry said in a soothing voice.

'Yes, well, are you going to stay here in the meantime? We're in no condition to fight Fleming off if he turns up here, which he is quite likely to do! And the phone seems to be dead!'

'Must have been a temporary fault,' Fry said, having picked up the receiver. 'It's working now.'

'I really think I'd like to go home,' Lillian said in a shaky voice. 'I just want to curl up in my own bed and try to forget that today ever happened.'

'Not a good idea,' Maudie murmured. 'That's the first place he'd look. Oh, where is Dick? Why doesn't he come? I really need him now!'

Another tap at the door caused the two

women to freeze. Fry flung it open to reveal Joan Blunt, resplendent in a floral frock and Sunday-best hat.

'Nurse Bryant! Mrs Grant! Are you all right?'

'It's a long story,' Maudie began.

'Never mind that now, my dear! I gather you've had a difficult time, and I've come to take you both to the vicarage. You'll be safe there with us. Your hubby sent somebody round with a message. He says he'll be along later.'

'By the look of you, you're in the middle of something important,' Maudie said. 'I wouldn't want to intrude.'

Mrs Blunt smiled. 'It's a joint meeting of representatives of the Women's Institute and the Mothers' Union,' she explained. 'Going at it hammer and tongs! It's about our Festival of Britain outing, as you may have guessed. Never mind that! I'll see you upstairs where you can lie down and have a nice cup of tea, and the ladies can carry on downstairs — 'carry on' being the operative phrase!'

'But I'm not Church of England,' Mrs Grant protested. 'I can't possibly come and stay in your house.'

Mrs Blunt laughed. 'Neither are half the women at the meeting, but we welcome all sorts under our roof, including friendly doggies named Rover!'

'Aarf!' said the dog, struggling to her side to receive the expected pat.

★　★　★

It was much later in the day when Maudie awoke to find Rover licking her face. Her mind had been in such a whirl that she hadn't expected to sleep, but somehow nature had taken over and bestowed its blessing on her, and now she felt refreshed and far more cheerful than when she'd arrived.

'Are you awake, old girl?' a familiar voice asked. She struggled to raise herself on one elbow.

'Dick! Is that you? What's going on? What time is it?'

'It's almost teatime. Are you dug in for the night, or do you mean to come home and get tea for a hungry man?'

'Oh. Yes, of course.'

Dick laughed. 'Only joking! Mrs Blunt has given us a pile of sandwiches left over from her meeting, and I know there's a tin of mulligatawny soup in the larder. All that will do me very nicely.'

'But what's happened? Have you caught Fleming? And where is poor Mrs Grant?'

'Fleming is all tucked up in a jail cell, and Mrs Grant has been driven home. Her neighbour, Mrs Lemmon, is sitting with her. I'll fill you in on everything later. Meanwhile, let's get you home and settled.'

Safe in the arms of her beloved Dick, Maudie felt the fearsome events of the day receding into the background. She allowed him to help her to her feet, and together they went downstairs to where Joan Blunt and the vicar were waiting.

'I'll see you tomorrow,' Mrs Blunt said, smiling. 'I'm sure you've lots to tell me!'

'Thank you so much,' Maudie said. 'I've had a lovely sleep. I shall be quite all right now.'

★　★　★

It was well into the evening before Maudie and Dick had time to exchange notes. They had eaten their meal, watched by the ever-hopeful Rover, who had declined to eat the dog food provided for him.

'I thought you said we should never feed him at the table,' Dick teased, as Maudie slipped yet another bread crust to their pet.

'Rover is a hero,' Maudie explained. 'Wounded in action! Someone should award him a medal after the way he tried to protect me from Fleming, so the least I can do is give him a little treat. Besides, he'll have to go to the vet tomorrow just to make sure he's all right. He could have broken ribs or something after the way that brute kicked him.'

'Good dog!' said Dick. 'Brave dog!' He was rewarded with a thump of Rover's tail.

'Now then, I want to hear all about Fleming!' Maudie said.

'You first, old girl.'

'Oh, all right. Is this an official interrogation?'

'I just have to get things in sequence. The boss will want to know.'

'Well, then, I went to Fred's cottage and waited for Mrs Grant to come . . . '

The clock on the wall ticked relentlessly as Maudie told her story. Dick listened without speaking, just giving a nod from time to time.

'And that's it, really,' she said at last. 'I think the most frightening part was when we were on the road, hoping to get here and barricade ourselves in before Fleming caught up with us. I kept hoping for somebody to come driving past so we could get help, but the road was deserted. Anyone would think that everyone had been abducted by aliens. In fact, even a glimpse of little green men would have been welcome under the circumstances!'

'I'm sure!'

'And that wasn't the end of it, Dick! I had to try to convince that loopy policewoman that something was wrong. She always makes me feel as if I'm a naughty schoolgirl, on the verge of hysterics.'

Dick laughed. 'Oh, that's just her

manner. She's all right, really. And she did pass on your message right away, and the boss and I swung into action and got a team of men on the road.'

'She could have told me that!' Maudie grumbled.

'There wasn't much to tell at that point. When we reached the cottage there was no sign of you or Fleming.'

'That's because we legged it as soon as Lillian coshed him! And you know the rest. But what happened to Fleming?'

'He had a car, hidden in the woods beside the glebe. When he came to, he apparently staggered off to retrieve it. Then he passed out again and our lads caught up with him when he was just sitting there, head down on the steering wheel. They had him in handcuffs while he was still groggy.'

21

'And that's more or less the whole story,' Maudie told Joan Blunt the next day. 'We were under siege until Constable Fry came to get us, and then you took us all under your wing.'

'Poor Mrs Grant must have been thinking two ways about believing Fleming was dead,' Mrs Blunt said, her homely face creased in sympathy. 'I mean, she must have been glad to have a crack at him, knowing he'd killed her brother. Who wouldn't be?'

'I don't think that occurred to her at the time. She needed to come to my rescue, and she just grabbed the nearest thing that came to hand and walloped him with it. She was overcome with remorse afterwards in case she'd killed him. At least, I think that's what it was. It may just have been fear of the hangman's noose.'

'Really, Nurse! What a way to put it!

You've been reading too many detective novels!'

'So what?' Maudie said, grinning. 'You know you can't resist them yourself!'

'But why did the wretched man turn to murder in the first place? Does anybody know?'

'Needless to say, Fleming isn't talking, but apparently he's being investigated in banking circles. Dick has the idea that Linnie Jenkins — that's the girl in Wales whose money he stole — won't have been the only one he defrauded. Being in banking, he probably had better than usual opportunities to separate people from their money. Indeed, it may turn out that he's been embezzling funds from the bank itself.'

'And where does poor Fred come in?'

'Having recognized Fleming, it would simply have been a matter of time before he went to the police with his suspicions, hoping to obtain justice for Linnie. I'm sure he knew nothing about any subsequent goings-on, but Fleming would have known that once an investigation was started, the whole story would come out.

Fred had to be killed before he could talk.'

'And you and Mrs Grant?'

'We don't know for sure, but Dick thinks we were just in the wrong place at the wrong time. He probably came to Fred's place to see if he could find any incriminating evidence the police had missed, or didn't recognize as such. Letters, perhaps; correspondence between Fred and the young woman. Although it wasn't likely that the police would have overlooked anything, I suppose he couldn't afford to take that chance.'

'And if he hadn't come across the pair of you there, I suppose a visit to Mrs Grant's house would have been next on his list!' Rover sidled up to Mrs Blunt, his tongue hanging out. 'Who's a boofuls boy, then?' she asked, ruffling his fur with a loving hand. 'Have you had him to the vet? Is he all right? Rover, I mean; not the vet!'

'Dick took him over first thing this morning. There's nothing radically wrong; just a bit of bruising, Mr Bradley thinks. He'll be all right in a day or two.'

'Thank goodness for that! Are you ready for a cuppa now? And a slice of my bran loaf to go with it? Fresh-baked this morning, with dates in it!'

'How can I refuse an offer like that?' Maudie said. 'By the way, what happened about the bus trips they were discussing yesterday?'

Mrs Blunt pulled a face. 'All sorted, thank goodness! They're putting on two outings after all, open to anybody who cares to come, so as to make up the numbers.'

'And where are they going? Somewhere nice?'

'The WI lot are going over to Frampton to see a pageant in the grounds of Frampton House. A number of WI branches are taking part in an extravaganza called Britain Through the Ages. You know the sort of thing, Nurse. People in costume swan onto the stage while a narrator with a megaphone explains what they're meant to represent. Then they walk off and another lot take their place.'

'I see. And the Mothers' Union? What delights have they plumped for?'

'Oh, they've gone in for something a bit more highbrow. They're off to Stratford to see a play. At first it was going to be *King Lear*, but a couple of the women thought that would be too heavy going, so now they've booked *The Tempest*. I prefer *A Midsummer Night's Dream* myself, but apparently it wasn't on offer, at least not on any of the dates when we could get the bus.'

'So it's business as usual in Llandyfan,' Maudie remarked. 'I can't say I'm sorry to see things return to normal. I can do without so much excitement in my condition.'

'And you're sure that all is well with you and the baby after yesterday?' Mrs Blunt asked.

'Never better. Oh, Dick wanted to rush me off to Doctor Dean, but if my headlong flight down the lane yesterday didn't shake anything loose, I'm sure nothing will! No, I shall just potter round the house for the next little while, enjoying the peace and quiet until it's time for me to go into The Elms.'

'There was one funny thing this

morning,' Mrs Blunt said slowly. 'I'd rinsed through a few undies by hand, and was outside hanging them out when I noticed somebody wandering around the graveyard. I thought it might be a stranger wanting help; you know how enthusiasts come here hoping to do brass rubbings in the church. So I went out to introduce myself.'

'You mean you just wanted to know what was going on!' Maudie chortled.

Mrs Blunt blushed. 'Well, that too, I must admit. Anyway, you'll never guess who it was! That RSPCA man who found Mr Woolton's body!'

'John Landry.'

'Was that his name? I'd forgotten. He said he wondered if Mr Woolton had been buried yet. He wanted to pay his respects, since he was the one who had discovered the body in the first place. That is, if you don't count your Rover!'

Maudie frowned. 'That's funny. I mean, I can understand why he might want to attend the funeral, but why come all the way over here on the bus when he could have telephoned the vicar? What did you tell the man?'

'Oh, I said that as far as I knew Fred's remains were still at the mortuary, and that when the time came the interment would probably be in the Methodist graveyard, not here. Mrs Grant hasn't mentioned anything of the sort to you, has she?'

'Nothing at all.'

'Oh, well, I suppose your hubby will put you in the picture when the time comes. And will you let me know when he does, in case we have other enquiries here?'

'Will do. Now, I think I'll go back home and put my feet up. Thanks for the tea, and your bran loaf was delicious. You must let me have the recipe some time.'

★ ★ ★

'Drat!' Maudie told Rover when they were turning in at her garden gate. 'I forgot to tell Mrs Blunt that your master has heard back from Canada, and the search for Godfrey Woolton is on! Oh, well, I suppose it will keep for another day!'

Rover, busy investigating an intriguing smell at the gatepost, made no reply. Maudie's thoughts went back to what Dick had told her the previous evening.

'They're looking for drivers' licenses first. That may turn up something.'

'Yes, there can't be too many Godfrey Wooltons over there, can there?'

'The thing is, though, my pals only have access to Ontario records. The other provinces have their own registries. We might have better luck if the chap has done something criminal.'

'Dick! Don't even joke about such a thing. Poor Mrs Grant has enough on her plate without finding out that her long-lost brother is a crook!'

'I'm only saying!'

'Well, don't! What I'm hoping for is that Godfrey is an upstanding citizen who wants nothing more than to be reunited with his little sister. And that he has a large family who will be a comfort to her in her old age.'

'It's a lovely thought, old girl, but you

mustn't bank on it. If Woolton really wanted to know, don't you think he would have started to search for his brother and sister by now? Perhaps he only wants to look forward, not back. Come to that, he might have died years ago. After all, what chance did a twelve-year-old child have, cast off somewhere in the wilds of Canada at the turn of the century?'

'We'll just have to wait and see, won't we?' Maudie knew that Fred had attempted to trace his brother with the help of the Salvation Army, although nothing had come of that as far as Lillian Grant knew. Was that because Godfrey Woolton did not wish to be found; or, worse yet, was already dead? Maudie preferred to think that the lack of success was only due to the intervention of the war.

The Salvation Army had enough to do trying to reunite families torn apart by the conflict. She had heard many tragic stories in her work as a nurse. Sometimes men had returned from serving in the armed forces only to find that their homes had been destroyed by the bombing and their wives were missing. And what if those wives did not wish to be found? And in some cases young children, evacuated to country places for their own safety, had been orphaned when their parents had been killed in action, or during the Blitz. Occasionally post-war searches had ended in tragedy. Maudie had been involved in one such case when she had stumbled upon the body of a man who had come to Llandyfan in search of a missing grand-child.

'Forget all that!' she said aloud. 'Come on, Rover, in we go. Bikkies!'

Delighted with the prospect, the dog abandoned his task and followed her into the house.

22

Following Maudie's terrible experience with Basil Fleming, Dick insisted that she take things very quietly for the remaining weeks of her pregnancy. 'It could so easily have gone wrong!' he said. 'I dread to think what could have happened if Mrs Grant hadn't had the presence of mind to wallop the wretched man with that warming pan! And on top of that, running home as you did has probably done you no good at all!'

'Come on, Dick!' she protested. 'It's not as if I got involved with the chap on purpose! All I did was to go along with Lillian while she tidied up her brother's things. How were we to know that Fleming would turn up with all guns blazing?'

'Yes, and I shouldn't have let you even do that! From now on, you leave the police work to the experts and mind your own business. Is that clear?'

For once, Maudie didn't feel like arguing. She was at that state of pregnancy where she just wanted to exist in a dreamlike state, waiting quietly for her baby to arrive. Dick tried to make her go to see Dr Dean, just to make sure that everything was as it should be, but she did object to that. She was well aware of any warning signs that might appear, and so far there was nothing to worry about. As a midwife, she felt entitled to pull rank!

'All right, but at the slightest sign of anything amiss, you must phone me at work and I'll rush home at once, do you understand? The boss has children of his own. I know he won't make a fuss if I have to leave in a hurry.'

'That's a laugh! I always get through to the dragon lady. I certainly don't feel like explaining my symptoms to a bossy policewoman.'

'Never mind about her! I'll make sure she understands that if you do happen to call she's to connect you with me at once, or I'll know the reason why!'

'Right-ho!'

'And another thing. You're not to lift anything heavy. No dragging the Hoover upstairs or taking the heavy dustbin out. Leave all that sort of thing to me.'

Maudie sighed. 'Don't fuss, Dick! I know what I'm doing!' She supposed that she ought to be glad that he cared.

★ ★ ★

She spent her days alternately sitting with her feet up and taking gentle strolls in the fresh air. Now was the time to finish knitting the baby's pram suit — and it was driving her mad! She had done the leggings first because putting the feet in made for interesting work, with a certain amount of decreasing and increasing. The helmet, too, had been interesting to knit. The jacket was another matter. The rows in the back and sides had seemed to go on forever, and making the thing up wasn't as easy as she'd expected. Maybe it was the bouclé wool that had something to do with it; all those knobbly bits tended to get in the way of her bodkin. Now there was just the collar left to do;

for that, she had to pick up stitches along the neck, and somehow it was turning out to be lopsided. Muttering a curse, she pulled out the stitches and began again. Then she pushed the whole thing into her knitting bag. Out of sight, out of mind! She would take it with her to the nursing home. It would give her something to do while she was convalescing.

She turned her attention to a slim volume entitled *Name Your Child*, given to her by Joan Blunt. They had discussed names but hadn't reached any conclusion. Dick had finally come up with the idea that they should wait until the baby was actually here and they could see what it looked like.

'Does anybody really look like their name?' she asked, rather bewildered by the idea.

'I don't know about that, but I do know people whose names don't suit them at all.'

'Oh, nobody likes their own name,' Maudie said. 'When I was growing up I always wished I'd been called Vivienne or Felicity.'

'If it's a boy, we should give him a distinguished name, don't you think? A name he can live up to.'

'Hannibal, you mean, or Napoleon?'

'Well, I'm not sure I'd go that far, old girl. What do you think of Conrad?'

Maudie pulled a face. 'I'd prefer Hannibal.' The subject was dropped.

★ ★ ★

'I've had a transatlantic call at work,' Dick said one evening. 'From my old mate in Toronto. They think they may have located Godfrey Woolton over there.'

'In Toronto?'

'No, in a place called Medicine Hat, Alberta. A couple of the guys have been going through business directories in their off-duty time, and this chap has a used-car business out West.'

'Doing up classic cars, do you mean?'

'I doubt it. Over there it usually means a place where you can buy second-hand cars, the sort of vehicle people get rid of when they buy a later model. That doesn't matter, anyway. What is important is that they've found this chap and they're going to get in touch.'

'Are you going to let Lillian know?'

'Not yet, and I don't want you dropping any hints, either. We don't want to get her hopes up until we know more. Besides, even if this is her brother, he may not want to know.'

'Of course he'll want to know!'

Dick shook his head. 'It's a very sad thing, Maudie, but a lot of the people who went out there as kiddies feel there's a stigma attached to being an orphan immigrant. Some of them were treated well by the families they went to, but others were badly done by and taunted by other children. It was terribly unfair, but many have grown up feeling they were more or less second-class citizens. If this Godfrey has married, he may have kept his background a secret from any children and grandchildren. Now, if he admits to having a sister that nobody knew about, the whole sad story will have to come out.'

'Well, I jolly well hope he does the right thing!' Maudie muttered. 'Poor Lillian could do with some support after all she's been through!'

'I agree, but I'm not too hopeful. If Woolton was at all interested in finding his family, wouldn't he have done something about it a long time ago, starting from his end?'

'Perhaps it wouldn't have been easy from thousands of miles away,' Maudie said. 'It took Fred ages to track down his sister, and they were both in Britain.'

'We'll just have to sit back and wait and see what happens next, I suppose,' Dick told her.

But Maudie wasn't patient by nature, and right at the moment she seemed to be doing nothing else but wait for momentous things to happen! The young mothers in her care had often complained about how fed up they were towards the end of their pregnancies. Tired of enduring backache, tired of lugging extra weight around, tired of being unable to do up their own shoelaces! She had always nodded and smiled and told them that the end was in sight, and it would all be worth it when they had a lovely baby in their arms, but now she knew exactly how they felt!

And she did so long for a happy ending for Lillian Grant! The school holidays were about to start, and the woman's daughter was coming down from Manchester, where she taught eight-year-olds, to console her mother. Fred's funeral was due to take place soon, and after that the long process of healing could begin for them. If Godfrey Woolton entered the picture that would be marvellous!

Maudie hoped that she might be able to attend the funeral, although it would be touch and go if it was held too close to her due date. She, too, needed closure after her involvement in the investigation. She wondered where Basil Fleming would be tried for his crimes. Well, she certainly wouldn't be attending the proceedings, because she'd have a new baby to look after by then. Lillian might wish to be there, of course; justice must be seen to be done.

And although the finer points of the police findings had to be kept quiet until the trial, the *Midvale Chronicle* had printed several big stories under banner headlines dealing with Fleming's alleged fraudulent activities. *Banking Scandal! The Pensioners Con Man Duped!*

Having nothing better to do, Maudie clipped out these pieces and pasted them into her scrapbook, along with accounts of other cases in which she'd been involved. In years to come, she could show them to her child as proof that Mummy had helped to foil killers.

On learning that Maudie had been attacked by Fleming, an enterprising journalist had attempted to interview her for a national newspaper, but she had seen him off by turning her garden hose on him. Drenched and furious, he had shouted something about the public's right to know, but she had gone inside and shut the door, and he had not returned. 'That should dampen his enthusiasm!' she'd told Rover. Luckily for her, dogs cannot understand bad puns.

23

The day of the Women's Institute outing to Frampton-under-Lyme dawned without a cloud in the sky. By eight o'clock, when the bus drew up in front of the parish hall, the temperature had already risen to an uncomfortable level with worse to come. Maudie, standing at her front room window to catch a glimpse of the participants heading for the bus, felt hot and sticky. At least the weather was fine for the pageant, which was to be held outdoors in the grounds of the stately home. At any other time she might have enjoyed the event, but it was out of the question now.

By eleven o'clock the atmosphere was close, and Maudie found herself hoping for a thunderstorm to clear the air — although she usually detested storms, being afraid that her cottage might be struck by lightning and destroyed by fire. She hadn't worried about such a possibility when she only rented the place, but now that she and Dick were homeowners, it put a different complexion on the matter.

Rover was stretched out on the scullery floor where he apparently found some relief on the cool flagstones. She thought she might leave him there while she strolled over to the church. The ancient stone building was always cool in summer, and tended to be uncomfortably cold in winter. She would sit for a while and think peaceful thoughts, probably uninterrupted because the cleaners and the flower ladies would have gone on the bus trip.

Selecting a pew about half-way down on the right-hand side of the aisle, she squeezed herself in and sat. After murmuring a brief prayer, she looked around her. She always felt at peace in St John's. The glorious stained-glass windows, the memorial brasses, the altar with its snowy white cloth, the flowers on the windowsills; all were dear and familiar.

She noted with some surprise that the little door leading to the belfry was slightly ajar. It was usually kept locked in case some exploring child tried to get in and climb the narrow, winding stair that led up to the great bells. It was possible to climb out onto the roof from there — just the sort of thing a careless small boy might try to do, at great risk to his safety. Perhaps the sexton was up there doing something or other.

Now there were footsteps on the stair. Maudie looked up from her contemplation of the new tapestry kneeler in front of her, a luxury that was of no use to her in her present condition. To her dismay, it was not Pratt who appeared in the doorway, but John Landry. What on earth had he been up to? This wasn't even his church; he lived in Midvale, Surely he hadn't been thinking of killing himself by hurling himself off the church tower?

She put one hand over her face in an attitude of prayer, hoping that he would assume she was petitioning the Lord and should not be disturbed. She glanced at her wristwatch. A minute or two ticked by.

It was then that he noticed Maudie.

After a moment's hesitation he came towards her. 'Good morning, Mrs Bryant,' he said, in the hushed tone appropriate to their surroundings. 'Mind if I join you?'

'Yes I do, actually,' Maudie told him. What was the matter with the man? There were enough empty seats to accommodate a hundred people, so why did he have to sit next to her? It was as if he hadn't heard. He slid into the pew beside her, cutting off her retreat. She felt a frisson of fear.

'This is a grand old church, isn't it?' he remarked. 'Lucky to have escaped the bombing in the war, I'd say.'

'Yes, indeed.'

'It's amazing that so many of them are left standing, isn't it? When you think of places like Coventry and London, I mean. They really took a pasting.'

Maudie could smell his breath. He seemed to have been eating too many eggs. Still, this was no time to worry about the chap's diet. 'I must go,' she said. 'Do you mind letting me pass?'

He didn't move, and she couldn't escape because there was a pillar at the other end of the pew. 'I thought we might have a little chat,' he told her. 'After all, we do have something in common.'

'Do we?'

'Of course we do! The body in the glebe. I'll never forget that if I live to be a hundred. And that nice little dog; what became of him?'

With some relief Maudie heard the vestry door creak, and a moment later the Revered Harold Blunt entered the church.

'Ah, the vicar! I must be off or I shall miss my bus!' Landry announced, sliding out of the pew and retreating to the main door.

Maudie found herself shaking. 'Mr Blunt!' she called. 'Can you spare a minute, please?' She needed the reassurance of a friendly presence. The vicar slid into the pew in front of hers and turned to face her.

'Can I help you, Nurse? It's not your — er — time, is it? Should I ring for an ambulance?'

'No, no. That man . . . I was just a bit frightened. Silly, really, but he had me hemmed in and I suppose I panicked a bit.'

'That is only to be expected after your unfortunate experience with Mr Woolton's killer,' the vicar murmured, 'but the fellow is in police custody now so there is nothing to worry about.'

'Oh, I know that. But there's something spooky about that Landry. And what was he doing in the belfry? That's what I'd like to know.'

'Landry. Landry. That name sounds familiar, but I'm not quite sure . . . I don't think he's one of my parishioners, you know.'

'He isn't. He's that RSPCA man from Midvale who found Fred Woolton's body. This is the third time he's been here, to my knowledge. Mrs Blunt found him wandering round the graveyard the other day, and he couldn't give a satisfactory explanation of what he was doing there.'

'I believe my wife did mention something of the sort.'

'So now he's back here again. Why does he keep turning up? That's what I'd like to know!'

'Perhaps you should have a word with your husband, Nurse. You'll probably find that your Mr Landry is a respectable worker for the RSPCA, and simply a man with an interest in church architecture.'

'I don't think he's actually employed by them. He's just an animal lover who helps out when they have their flag day.'

'Ah, well, he's gone now. Nothing for you to worry about. It's only natural for you to feel a little emotional in your — um — condition. I suggest you go home, make yourself a nice cup of tea, and forget all about it. Would you like me to walk you home?'

'No, thank you; I shall be quite all right.' Silly old buffer! Emotional, indeed! She'd give him emotion! To her dismay, she felt hot tears springing to her eyes. With a gasp she pulled herself upright and stumbled out of the church, leaving the vicar open-mouthed behind her.

Rover opened one eye when he heard her come in. He thumped his tail and then, satisfied, went back to sleep. Obviously all was well here, or Rover would have behaved differently, but she still felt compelled to search all the rooms in case Landry was lurking there. There was no reason why he should be, of course; her rational mind told her that. Perhaps the vicar was right and her hormones were responsible for this feeling of unease; yet she couldn't seem to let go of her suspicion that something wasn't quite right.

* * *

The storm came up at five o'clock, just when Maudie was beginning her preparations for their evening meal. Not that there was much to do; in this heat, nobody wanted cooked food. She washed a few leaves of lettuce, and sliced cucumber and tomatoes. Dick wasn't overly fond of salad, preferring more solid food. Should she boil a few potatoes to make potato salad? Put together one or two devilled eggs? No, it was too much of an effort. It would be easier to open a tin of Dick's favourite corned beef and give him a few slices of that. As for herself, a poached egg on toast with a small side salad would satisfy her needs.

She felt a sudden longing for ice cream, preferably the kind with three colours included in the brick. Only the thought of the energy needed to drag herself to the village shop and back convinced her that she didn't need it as badly as all that.

The sky darkened and the thunder started to roll. She winced when the kitchen lit up with a great flash of forked lightning. Rover whined and disappeared under the table. Wartime recollections of cowering in the cupboard under the stairs during an air raid came to mind. She put down her knife and went into the living-room, where she pulled the curtains across the window before sitting down in a chair as far away from the glass as possible.

Suddenly the rain came thumping down, and with it came the scent of damp soil and flowers as the parched earth opened up to receive it. The heatwave had broken.

24

'Sorry I'm late home, love,' Dick said, planting a smacking kiss on Maudie's cheek. 'I got tied up and didn't have access to a phone, or I would have let you know.'

'It's all right; it's just a cold meal. What happened? Not another murder, I hope.'

'No, no, but it was something we had to look into right away. There's been another arson attempt on a church; a Methodist chapel at Brookfield. A lovely old place that is reputed to have been visited by John Wesley himself when he came to preach to the congregation. This is getting beyond serious, old girl. We've got to catch up with this firebug soon. So far only church buildings have been destroyed, and tragic though that may be, bricks and mortar can be replaced. But it's only a matter of time before someone gets killed. I shouldn't think this bloke goes inside to make sure the place is empty before he does his dirty work. What would he say if anyone noticed him? 'Everybody out, quick sharp, I'm going to set fire to the place!'?' Dick's mouth turned down in an expression of worry and disgust.

'Did they manage to save this chapel?'

'Fortunately, yes. The rain came pelting down in the nick of time and put out the worst of the flames even before the fire brigade arrived.'

'I suppose the place couldn't have been struck by lightning?' Maudie wondered. 'It was pretty fierce for a while. I know it gave me the jitters.'

Dick shrugged. 'We'll have to wait for the official report to find out. That rain turned out to be good news and bad news. It saved the chapel, but it meant there were no onlookers who might have noticed something. And of course we always keep a sharp eye out when a crowd gathers, in case the arsonist is standing around admiring his handiwork.'

'I'm sure you'll get to the bottom of it before much longer,' Maudie said. 'Well, I'll go and dish up. It'll be on the table by the time you've washed your hands.'

'Good, I'm starving!' Dick said as he headed for the stairs.

★ ★ ★

The Women's Institute members returned from their trip to Frampton in high spirits. Mrs Blunt called round the following morning and handed Maudie a small paper bag.

'This is for you, Nurse. I wish you could have been with us, but as you weren't I thought a little gift was in order.'

'How kind! Thank you very much. How did it all go? I hope you weren't soaked? The rain came down in torrents here.'

'Luckily it didn't start until we were on the way back. The driver had to stop the bus for a good ten minutes because the wipers just couldn't handle the onslaught. Aren't you going to look at your present?'

Maudie opened the bag and drew out an Irish linen tea towel. 'It's lovely,' she said. 'Much too good to use on wet crockery! I shall hang it on the wall instead.'

'As you can see, it's got flowers of Britain on it,' Mrs Blunt said. 'They had some with pictures of the big house, but as you weren't there to see the real thing I thought it wouldn't mean much to you, and I know you like flowers.'

'I do. And how was the actual pageant?'

'The organizers must have gone to a lot of trouble to make sure everyone got their fifteen minutes of fame. Each scene had one or two main characters, such as Elizabeth the First and Sir Francis Drake, accompanied by a lot of what Harold calls spear-carriers. The highlight of the day came when a teenaged girl rode in on a rather skittish horse; something to do with the Civil War, I think. Just in front of where I was sitting, there was a small boy who seemed bored with the whole thing. For some reason he had a small terrier with him, and just as the girl arrived he let go of the dog, which ran out in front of the horse, yapping. The horse reared up, the girl was thrown, and the horse galloped off with the Scottie in hot pursuit. I swear that child did it on purpose!'

'I hope the girl was all right?'

'Oh, the St John Ambulance people were right there to look after things, and I caught a glimpse of her later in the day, buying ice cream from the Wall's van. But would you believe it, Nurse, there were some people who thought the whole thing was staged? 'Jolly good, wasn't it, that scene,' I heard one woman say to her friend. 'It's so clever how they can train animals to do tricks like that.' Honestly, some people!'

'There's nowt so queer as folk.' Maudie quoted the old North Country adage.

'And apropos of that,' Mrs Blunt said, 'I gather from my husband that you had a rather unpleasant encounter with that Landry chap yesterday; in the church, no less!'

'I did, and I must admit that it rattled me a bit. If the vicar hadn't come in when he did, I don't know what might have happened.'

'You're not saying he might have . . . well, I don't know what I mean.

220

Robbed you, perhaps?'

'He could hardly have done that when I didn't have my handbag with me. All I had was my door key, and that was hidden in my skirt pocket. No, there's just something about him that makes me feel uncomfortable, and I'd like to know what he thought he was doing in the belfry.'

'I don't know what we should do if he comes back again,' Mrs Blunt said. 'Harold says we mustn't think of forbidding him to come into the church, which is there for everyone. What if he has some anxiety that's dragging him down, or perhaps he has something weighty on his conscience? He may be trying to summon up the courage to speak to a man of the cloth; or at least, that's what Harold says.'

'Then why doesn't he talk to one of the clergy in Midvale, where he lives?'

'Perhaps whatever is on his mind is so awful that he doesn't want anyone in his own town to know about it,' Joan Blunt suggested. The two women looked at each other in pleasurable surmise.

Maudie felt that she really should take herself in hand. No more dwelling on recent difficulties! For the sake of the baby, she must cultivate serenity: adopt a Madonna-like pose. If the child in her womb could sense the upheaval in her mind, that would not be a good thing. She must focus her thoughts on the baby instead, and the happiness that she hoped the future would bring.

With any luck, the child would grow up in a peaceful environment. Maudie herself had lived through two world wars, and she hoped she'd never see another one. The first time round she'd been a small child, scarcely able to understand what it was all about. In the second war she'd been a nurse, working in the Llandyfan district as a midwife, but getting there hadn't been easy. What a row there had been at home when she announced her intention to train as a nurse! Her parents had wanted her to leave school at the earliest possible opportunity and go into service as some sort of housemaid.

'Nursing!' her mother had said, looking horrified. 'You listen to me, my girl! You don't want to go into some hospital. They'll have you skivvying around after all those doctors, and who knows what awful diseases you'll pick up in those wards? You let me find you a place in some respectable household where you can work your way up to becoming a cook or a ladies' maid. Nursing is not for people like us.'

Maudie ignored all the doom-saying and applied to the hospital of her choice. While she was waiting to be admitted, she took a job in the greengrocer's round the corner from her home, and her parents had approved of that. It was good honest work and her employer was kind, but after one freezing winter spent arranging Brussels sprouts and cabbages in racks outside the shop, she had had enough.

Added to that, there was Billy Clark! Two years Maudie's junior, he was a spotty youth with a prominent Adam's apple who worked at the corn chandler's next door. His mission in life was to persuade Maudie to go to the picture palace with him. Hers was to avoid him without being unnecessarily unkind. Their mothers had been friends since their schooldays, and when they began to hint that their children might make a go of it, Maudie was horrified. To cries of outrage coming from all sides, she took herself off to the hospital to begin her training.

She had thoroughly enjoyed her career, and believed that she had been a useful member of society. How different her life would be today if she had stayed at home and lived her mother's dream! Maudie's faithful swain had eventually married Dulcie, the girl who had taken her place in the greengrocer's, and she'd hoped they'd found happiness together. But Billy had been called up when war was declared, and he had eventually been killed while serving in North Africa. His wife was now struggling to support herself and their six children.

'That could have been me,' Maudie told Rover, who listened with his head on one side. She really should stop confiding in the animal as if he were a person! Left alone in the cottage all day with only the dog for company, she had drifted into the habit without being aware of it.

'Who's a boofuls boy, then?' she asked. 'Does he want a bikkie?'

Rover whined softly in agreement.

25

Maudie was close to her time when the next shock came. 'What with one thing and another, I'll be lucky if this child isn't born with two heads!' she told Joan Blunt afterwards.

Her friend laughed gently. 'You thrive on excitement, Nurse, you know you do! And I'm sure that Baby Bryant is cast in the same mould, and can't wait to burst onto an unsuspecting world and start solving crimes like Mum and Dad!'

'Perhaps you're right, but I can tell you I really thought I was going mad when I saw that man on my doorstep!'

Maudie had been dozing in her armchair one afternoon, half-wondering if she could persuade Dick to take her to the Royal Oak for a pub supper if he got home in time. The heatwave had returned and she felt sticky and lethargic. When the doorbell rang, she moved restlessly in her chair. The caller was probably only somebody selling something. Could she stay where she was and pretend there was nobody in? But the trouble with that little idea was that she would be perfectly visible if the caller was rude enough to peer in through the living-room window which was just to the left of the door.

'Just coming!' she called, struggling out of her chair. The door had swollen in the heat, and she had to use all her strength to tug at it. By the time she had it open, she was prepared to give the unlucky salesman short shrift, but then the world seemed to spin around her when she saw Fred Woolton standing on the step.

'Are you all right, Ma'am? I surely didn't mean to startle you,' he said, in what she thought might be an American accent. She swayed, clutching the doorpost for support.

'I'm so sorry, I'll be all right in a minute,' she muttered, trying to calm her rapidly-beating heart. But why was she apologizing? It wasn't her fault that her erstwhile milkman seemed to have come back from the dead!

'I'm Godfrey Woolton,' he said, holding out his hand.

'How do you do, Mr Woolton. I suppose you'd better come in.' She stood aside to let him enter, indicating an upright chair standing near the armchair she had just vacated. 'I'm so sorry. That didn't sound very gracious, did it? It's just that it was just a shock, seeing you here. I thought for a minute you were Fred, you see. Not that I believe in ghosts, but . . . well, you do resemble him!'

Now that she had calmed down, she could see that the two men were not all that much alike. There was a certain facial resemblance, but where Fred had been wiry and slightly stooped — years of bending over to deposit milk bottles on doorsteps had done that to him, she supposed — Godfrey was definitely running to fat. Then, too, his hair was done in a brownish-grey brush cut, while Fred's pate had been balding. Woolton seemed to be waiting for her to say something more. 'They found you, then,' she murmured, feeling silly.

'They did indeed, Ma'am.' He launched

into a long litany of names and places and organizations that meant nothing to her, but she let him ramble on while she tried to gather her wits. 'I was devastated to learn about poor Freddie,' he concluded, 'but overjoyed that our Lillian has been found. I dropped everything and hopped on a plane at once, and here I am. Fourteen hours it took me to get over here on a turbo-prop, with a stop off at Gander, Newfoundland and another in Reykjavik, but here I am now. I hired a car at the airport and drove nonstop across country, not wanting to waste any time.'

'And have you seen Mrs Grant yet?'

'Well, no. I didn't have an exact address for her, just this place, Llandyfan.' He pronounced it as 'Clandy-fan', but she didn't trouble to correct him. 'So when I got here, I asked for directions at the store, and the lady in charge of the post office told me to call on you first. You are the local nurse, she tells me, and a friend of my sister. Best not to spring myself on Lillian unannounced, in case it gave her a coronary.'

I'll swing for that Mrs Hatch! Maudie

thought. Of course, she was right about Lillian, but what about me? I'm the one who's in a delicate condition! 'I'm sure Mrs Grant will be overjoyed to see you,' she said carefully, 'but I do agree that it might be wise to give her some warning.'

'Then can you call her up, Ma'am? Break the news to her gently?'

'I'm afraid she isn't on the phone, Mr Woolton.'

'Not on the phone? What kind of one-horse town is this, anyway?'

'A quiet country place slowly recovering from six years of war, Mr Woolton. We don't have all the amenities you've no doubt been used to.'

'Then what are we going to do?'

A longing to be in on the great reunion overcame Maudie's good sense, and she smiled brightly at her visitor. 'If you take me to Mrs Grant's home, you can wait in the car while I pop inside to give her the good news. How will that suit you?'

'Sure! That would be great! Are you free to go now?' Maudie agreed that she was. Rover scrambled in ahead of her as she climbed slowly into the passenger side of his car. Woolton appeared not to notice the dog, and if he did, he probably thought it best not to complain when she was the necessary link between him and his long lost sister.

* * *

Luckily, Lillian was at home. Maudie didn't think she could have borne it if the dramatic scene had to be postponed, possibly with herself not part of the picture,

'Oh, it's you, Nurse! And the dear little doggie! Is he out for walkies, then?'

'May we come in? I've something to tell you, Mrs Grant.'

'Something nice, I hope!'

'The very best.'

Moments later, Rover looked on in some alarm as Lillian Grant sobbed and moaned, rocking back and forth on her chair. 'I can't believe it! After all these years, to find him at last! Oh, Mrs Bryant, can it really be true? When is he coming? Will he be here for Fred's funeral?'

'As a matter of fact, he's outside in the

car at this very moment,' Maudie said gently.

'What! Are you sure? Oh, I can't go and look! I haven't seen him for forty years! What if I don't recognize him?'

'Oh, you'll know him, all right,' Maudie told her. 'I'll pop out and send him in, then, shall I?'

'Yes, yes. Oh, my hair is a mess and I'm in my pinny! What on earth will he think of me?'

'He'll think you're as lovely as the flowers in May,' Maudie said, blinking back tears. She returned to the car, where she found Godfrey Woolton leaning on the bonnet.

'You can go in,' she told him.

'Aren't you coming too?'

'No, I think not.' Much as she longed to witness their reunion, she suddenly felt as if it would be a gross intrusion. She must back away and leave them to it.

'But how will you get home?'

'I'll walk. There's a short cut across that field there.'

'Well, if you're sure.'

She waited until he had disappeared

into the house and the door shut behind him, and then she strolled towards the glebe. If she took it gently, the walk would do her no harm at all, and she had always told her mothers-to-be that moderate exercise was good for them. There was no harm in taking her own advice!

★ ★ ★

'Unbelievable!' Dick said when Maudie gave him the news that evening. 'You mean the chap jumped on a plane just like that, and came all the way to Britain? The police over there barely had time to let him know we were searching for him, and now here he is!'

'When we were driving over to Lillian's he told me how he'd longed to get in touch with his family all these years, but he didn't know how to go about it. He was just a child when he was shipped out to Canada, and children don't always understand what is going on around them. He couldn't even recall the name of the place where the orphanage was, much less identifying details of his parents. He did make an attempt to trace his family in later years, but it came to nothing. Then the war intervened and people had other things to think about.'

'I see. And how is it that this Woolton could drop everything and come here at a moment's notice?'

'I gather he's a widower with grown-up sons. The boys are in business with him and will keep things humming along while he's away. And don't forget Fred's funeral. If the man was coming at all, he'd naturally want to be here for that. Being reunited with his sister is just a wonderful bonus. And I know she'll be glad of the support when the time comes to bury poor old Fred.'

Tears came to Maudie's eyes as she remembered Lillian's reaction to the news. Where murder was concerned, there could hardly be a happy ending; yet it had led to a brother and sister finding each other again, and that was some compensation.

26

Dick and the rest of the team had managed to uncover a fair amount of background information on Basil Fleming and his criminal acts. When Maudie complained about the long hours he was working, Dick explained that they wanted to build up a good case for the prosecution so there was no chance of Fleming getting off.

'But surely it's all cut and dried,' she protested. 'He was all set to bump off Lillian and me. And as far as poor Fred was concerned, you do have the murder weapon, don't you?'

'Yes, thanks to you. But we must still establish motive for Fred's killing. Defence counsel will do everything possible to get him off, and we must have a watertight case against the man.'

'Hanging is too good for him!' Maudie said fiercely.

'That's the point, though, old girl. In

235

this country, it's innocent until proven guilty. We can't run the risk of hanging an innocent man,'

'Innocent, my foot!'

'I know, I know, but we can't let up until we work out what Fleming has done with all the money he embezzled. He had many more victims than we thought at first. People are starting to come forward now to say they were defrauded by him. He offered to invest their money with high rates of return, only to tell them that the bottom fell out of their shares, or whatever they were. When they complained, they were told that there is always a risk in such ventures and there was nothing that could be done about it; their money had just melted away. Of course, Fleming never invested it at all. He simply gave them some worthless certificates and salted the money away for himself.'

'Are you saying that Fleming is a stockbroker, then?'

'Nothing of the sort. People trusted him because he was a banker. I can imagine the scene. Some pensioner comes to complain about the low rate of interest on his bit of savings. Fleming tells him he knows how he can do better and names a much better rate. 'Making a fast buck', they call it in Canada. The pensioner falls for the trick and pays up.'

'It beats me how people can be such fools!'

'Ah, but people tend to trust banks, Maudie. The average person doesn't know much about investments; do you? And if you went in and asked Arthur Ramsey how you could do better, wouldn't you believe what you were told?'

'I wouldn't go near that man with a ten-foot pole!'

'You don't like him because he was unkind to his wife when she had post-natal depression. That doesn't mean you wouldn't trust his judgment on banking affairs.'

'That's as maybe, but where is all the money Fleming stole from his clients? Is there any chance of their getting something back?'

'We have to find it first. We don't know where it has been stashed away, and

Fleming isn't talking. Even with his cunning, I doubt very much if it's been invested on the Swiss money market!'

★   ★   ★

Fred Woolton's funeral was held at the Methodist chapel on a cool summer day. It had rained during the night, and water was still dripping off the trees in the little graveyard when he went to his last rest. Maudie had thought it unwise for her to attend, being so near her time, but she felt that the Wooltons would understand, Joan Blunt was there, however, and she called at the cottage on her way home to tell Maudie about it.

'My dear, you should have seen the crowd! I must say, they gave Fred a good send-off.'

'Not sightseers, I trust?'

'Oh, no. I think they were genuine mourners. Fred was well-liked, and of course we all took our milk from him. I expect there was some sense of being there in support for Mrs Grant as well.'

'Not to mention wanting to have a

good look at the long-lost brother!'

'That's only natural, isn't it, Nurse? Everybody loves a story with a happy ending, if you can call it that, under the circumstances.'

★　★　★

One evening a week later, Godfrey Woolton called at the cottage to say goodbye. 'Going back to Canada, are you?' Dick asked. 'What about Mrs Grant? Will she be going too?'

'My niece is staying on with her for the rest of the school holidays. Lillian may come out to visit us next summer, if she can get up the nerve. She says she doesn't know which would be worse: a long airplane flight with the risk of coming down in the ocean, or the week-long journey by ship, being seasick all the way!' He laughed gently.

'Lillian must be so pleased to have found you,' Maudie murmured.

'I'll say she is! And Officer Bryant, you may like to know that we've learned what happened to our mother. Lillian received a letter from the Salvation Army folks just this morning. Mum died only five years ago, in a sanatorium in Bristol.'

'Tuberculosis?' Maudie suggested. 'How sad that you couldn't have traced her while she was still alive.'

'It sure is, but at least we know what became of her, otherwise we'd never have stopped wondering.'

* * *

'I can't imagine how that poor soul must have felt,' Maudie said later, when Godfrey Woolton had gone on his way. As a mother-to-be, she had a new perspective on the mother-and-child bond. 'Perhaps she always hoped that her situation would improve so she could reclaim her children; and then when it didn't, just imagine her pain, wondering where they were and if they were being well-treated.'

'And having handed them over to the authorities, she might have been glad to be free to make her own way without youngsters to provide for,' Dick said. He had seen and heard too much during his career in the police force to have any illusions about such matters.

'Dick Bryant! How can you be so unkind! That poor woman! I certainly hope you never say such a thing to Lillian Grant!'

'Don't be silly, of course I wouldn't. All I'm saying is that you can't impose sainthood on Mrs Woolton without knowing the facts. Not that it has anything to do with us now. And, sorry as I am for their sufferings, I know full well that such stories are commonplace. You know, Maudie, when they try to teach you history at school, it's all about battles and dates. They never tell you what becomes of the innocent victims of war. The Wooltons are just as much casualties as those people who were killed in the Blitz or on the field of battle.'

This gloomy thought was interrupted by a crash and the sound of breaking china. 'I'll swing for that cat!' Maudie yelped. 'That wretched animal! He's at it again!'

'Well, if you will leave the larder

window open, what do you expect?' Dick told her. 'No, don't get up. I'll go and see what's happened.'

A moment later, Rover shot through the living-room and up the stairs with a string of sausages hanging from his mouth.

'Dick!' Maudie bawled. 'He's got your supper!' She stifled a giggle as Dick charged up the stairs in pursuit of the criminal. Sounds of scuffling were heard overheard before Dick re-emerged, dragging the dog by the collar.

'He'd gone under the bed and I had the devil of a time dragging him out!' Dick muttered. 'These sausages don't seem to have come to any harm, though. Do you suppose they'd be all right if we gave them a good wash before putting them in the frying pan? We can't just throw them in the dustbin, and if we let Rover have them now it would be sending him quite the wrong message.'

'Bad dog!' Maudie scolded, trying not to notice the sorrowful look in the animal's eyes. 'I'll open a tin of corned beef for you, Dick, and mind you don't slip him a bit under the table! And we'll have none of your bachelor tricks here, thank you very much! I'll cook the sausages tomorrow and cut them up to mix in with his dog food, and perhaps he won't put two and two together. Meanwhile, it's hard tack for you tonight my lad, and lucky to get it!'

'Aarf!' said Rover.

27

Maudie swayed, clinging to the arm of a chair for balance.

'Here, are you all right?' asked Dick, alarmed.

'I'm just a bit dizzy. I'll be all right in a minute.'

'No you won't! You're white as a sheet. I'm calling Dr Dean!'

'I don't want to see a doctor! It's not the baby coming, if that's what you're afraid of.'

But Dick had already started to telephone and, apparently sweeping aside the protests of the doctor's receptionist, insisted that Maudie be seen at once.

'Right! Yes, Doctor! I will! Thank you! See you in a few minutes!'

'Now what have you done?' Maudie demanded. 'He's not coming here, is he? Look at the state of the place. I haven't had time to tidy up today, or vacuum, or anything.'

'I'm taking you over to Midvale. The doc says he would come here, but in case you have to be admitted to the nursing home it would be just as well to have you on the spot. Come on, no arguments. Let's get you in the car.'

'I'll just have to change my smock,' Maudie said. 'This one's all wrinkled.'

'Nonsense. You look perfectly all right as you are. Now, are you going to do as you're told, or do I have to carry you?'

'You'll give yourself a hernia if you do,' Maudie grumbled. 'All right, I'm coming. You don't have to be so masterful! Look, I'd better collect my sponge bag and a nightie, just in case.'

'I can bring whatever you might need later. Now come on!'

Truth be told, she did feel a bit groggy, so she allowed him to take her by the arm and out to the car. All the way to Midvale he kept up a non-stop monologue which she managed to ignore. Either he was extremely nervous, or this flow of chatter was designed to reassure the patient! Either way, she didn't feel it necessary to respond. Lulled by the movement of the car, she slept.

★　★　★

'Your blood pressure is raised significantly,' Dr Dean announced sternly. 'Do you believe there is any particular reason for that, Nurse?'

'It's true that I've been under some stress,' Maudie admitted.

'Have you put on more weight than usual? Are your ankles swollen at all?'

'It's been some time since I've been able to see my feet, Dr Dean, but no, they don't feel any different. And look, my hands and face aren't swollen at all.'

'They seem normal,' he said, bending down and placing a finger on one of her feet to see if it left an indentation. 'There's probably nothing to worry about, but I'll order a urine test, just to be on the safe side. You can go home for now, and I'll phone if I want to admit you.'

'Thank you, Doctor.'

★　★　★

'So what did he say?' Dick demanded. 'Are you all right? Is the baby . . . '

'Stop fussing, Dick! My blood pressure is up a bit; and no wonder, when I think about all that has happened this week! I've left a urine sample, and the doctor will bring me back in if there's any cause for concern.'

'Why? What does that mean?'

'It's a routine test to see if any protein is leaking into the urine.'

'Is that bad?'

Seeing that her husband wasn't to be fobbed off with platitudes, Maudie launched into a little lecture that she hoped would satisfy him.

'There is a condition known as pre-eclampsia, where blood pressure rises, fluid is retained and protein leaks into the urine. Treated promptly, it can prevent the problem developing into full-blown eclampsia, also known as toxaemia of pregnancy, which is serious.'

'And what does this treatment involve?'

'Oh, nothing very terrible. Bed rest, water pills, some form of blood pressure medication.' Maudie felt there was no need to burden Dick with what might go wrong if the prescribed treatment did not work. Indeed, she preferred to look on the bright side unless informed otherwise. She had seen some of her patients safely through pre-eclampsia to a successful outcome, and knew just what modern medicine could achieve.

When Dr Dean eventually telephoned, he sounded remarkably cheerful. In fact, his bedside manner was miles better than the arrogant face he presented to his colleagues in the medical world, as Maudie knew from experience!

'I don't think that anything is radically wrong,' he began. 'You're probably right when you attribute your hypertension to too much stress or excitement. But I do feel we should keep an eye on you, Nurse, in view of your advanced age.'

Charming! thought Maudie. Still, she knew what he meant. Forty-two was pretty ancient to be having a first child! Might as well admit it!

'That being the case, I would like to admit you to The Elms, where they can keep watch on your blood pressure, and see that you get plenty of rest. If anything changes, or if you've shown no sign of delivering by your due date, we can induce labour.'

'I see,' Maudie replied. There was no need for her to question his judgment, for she would have given similar advice to any patient of her own who might have been in like case.

'So I'll tell them to expect you, and you can turn up at any time after noon and get settled in.'

'Thank you, Dr Dean.'

In anticipation of a swift trip to the nursing home, her bags had been packed for some time now. All she needed to do was to pop in a few extra paperbacks and she'd be ready for the off. Baby Bryant's bag was also packed in readiness, with a complete set of tiny garments and two extra nappies 'in case'.

'This is a great relief to me,' Dick told her when she informed him of the arrangements.

'Why? I've already explained things to you. You really mustn't worry.'

'It isn't that, old girl. I've been thinking

about what would happen if you suddenly went into labour on a weekday, while I was at work. What if I was tied up somewhere out in the country where I couldn't be contacted. How would you get to Midvale then?'

'I suppose I might have dialled 999 and asked for an ambulance,' Maudie said, laughing at the horrified expression on his face.

'Well, now you won't have to. You'll be safely installed at The Elms when the balloon does go up.'

'I have never liked that expression,' Maudie muttered, 'and I like it even less in this context. I can imagine myself bursting wide open, helplessly watching Baby Bryant ascending to the ceiling, away from my waiting arms.'

'Fool!' Dick said, leaning over to kiss his wife. 'I'll go and phone right away, to let the chief know I must be back home by noon. In fact, I'd better make it earlier because of taking Rover over to the vicarage.'

'You won't need to take the whole afternoon off, either. You can just deposit me at the front door of The Elms and return to work like a good boy.'

'Spoilsport!'

'Perhaps you'd better phone the vicarage now,' Maudie said, 'to let the Blunts know you'll be coming. I haven't had a minute to let anybody know that we're under starter's orders.'

Dick scratched his head. With a thoughtful expression on his face, he said, 'You know, it's just beginning to sink in! By this time next week, or even sooner, we could be parents!'

'You mean you've only just realized that, Dick Bryant? What do you think I've been doing all these months buying baby clothes and getting bigger around the waistline?' Maudie looked at him in mock amazement.

'Oh, I know we've been expecting an addition to the family, of course I do,' Dick replied. 'But this will be a real little person, a new sprig on our family tree. Dependent on us, eventually smiling up at us and calling us Mum and Dad.'

'And bawling away half the night, and soaking its nappies and demanding food,'

Maudie reminded him with a grin.

'You can laugh all you want to, old girl, but it seems like a miracle to me. Dick Bryant, forty-five years of age, first-time father!'

'The arrival of a new baby is always a miracle,' Maudie said softly. 'I've held hundreds of them in my arms before handing them over to their mothers, but this time the baby will be mine to cherish. I can't wait to see what he or she looks like, whether it resembles either of us or just looks like itself.'

'Then I hope the poor kid doesn't have my nose,' Dick said ruefully. 'Especially if the baby turns out to be a girl.'

'I daresay she'll survive it if she does,' Maudie said lovingly, planting a kiss on the offending part of her husband's face. 'And speaking of noses, we'll have to make sure that Rover's isn't put out of joint when we bring the baby home.' At the sound of his name, the dog sprang to his feet and padded to her side. She patted him absently. It was almost time to leave for Midvale.

28

Maudie was given the two-bedded room that she had seen on her previous visit. 'You'll have it all to yourself for the moment,' she was told by the young nurse who admitted her. She wasn't sure whether she felt glad or sorry. A bit of company would have been nice; but on the other hand, she could play her little wireless or keep the reading lamp on at night without having to consider anyone else.

'It's too bad you don't have a room with a nice view,' the girl went on, as if the place was a luxury hotel that might be found wanting, 'but otherwise we're fully-booked.' Maudie already knew that her window overlooked the church next door, with only a narrow alleyway in between the two buildings.

'Oh, that's all right,' she said. 'I haven't come here for the view. I've brought my knitting and several books I've been meaning to re-read, so I'll be happy enough, I'm sure.'

'Right-ho, Mrs Bryant. Now, if you'd like to undress and slip into your nightie I'll be back in a tick to take your TPR and BP. That means your temperature, pulse and respiration,' she explained, 'and your blood pressure as well.'

'Thank you, I did know that,' Maudie told her.

'Oh, do you? That's good. Sometimes our patients get upset if we flood them with medical jargon. I find it's always best to explain before misunderstandings arise.'

'Absolutely,' Maudie replied. She hadn't told the staff about her profession, and she intended to let matters stay that way. Otherwise they might suspect that she was watching their every move with an eagle eye, ready to pounce and criticize. Here at The Elms, Midwife Maudie Bryant would be just another patient.

* * *

The day passed slowly. Muted sounds came to Maudie in her hospital bed: the distant wail of a discontented baby, the low-pitched laughter of passing nurses, the clatter of dishes somewhere below. It all sounded comforting and familiar. The evening brought visitors to the nearby rooms, but nobody came for Maudie. She had told Dick not to bother since she had only just arrived. A beaming man bounced in at one point, waving a bunch of carnations at her, before saying, 'Oops, sorry!' and beating a hasty retreat. A new father, she surmised, smiling.

Her evening meal was brought on a tray by a smiling foreigner in a pink overall. 'Very good, Madam. You like?'

Maudie peered at the dishes suspiciously. Some sort of shredded meat in gravy, accompanied by mashed potato and the inevitable boiled cabbage. A pepper pot, but no salt shaker because of her high blood pressure. A small dish of egg custard was the only pudding.

'I don't think I'll eat the cabbage,' she said, since some response seemed to be called for. 'It gives me wind just now.'

'Wind? You like me close the window, Madam?'

'Never mind,' Maudie said, baring her

teeth in what she hoped would be interpreted as a grateful smile. The pink lady departed.

Maudie tasted the fricassee and fretfully put down her fork. She had hoped it might be chicken, but no such luck. It was the despised corned beef, disguised by dark brown gravy. Dick would have eaten it with relish, but he wasn't here. He was probably at home, enjoying lovely, lovely fish and chips, smothered in salt and vinegar! Her mouth watered at the thought.

The night turned chilly. Maudie got up and went to feel the radiator, which was stone cold. She rang her bell and a nurse appeared at once.

'Is everything all right, Mrs Bryant? You're not feeling any contractions, are you?'

'I'm just a bit cold. How do I turn this thing on?'

'I'm afraid you don't, Mrs Bryant. The system is always turned off on the first of May, and not started up again until the first of October. Would you like me to fetch you a hot water bottle? And there's another blanket if you need it.'

'Thank you. That would be very kind.'

But despite these refinements, Maudie could not get to sleep. Perhaps it was the strange bed, or just the fact that she was missing Dick and her own home. She struggled up to turn on the bedside lamp, and reached for one of her paperbacks.

When she had read the first page three times without taking in the meaning of the words, she gave it up as a bad job and switched off the light. If she snuggled down and pondered happy thoughts, perhaps she'd soon nod off. But sleep still eluded her.

At two o'clock she was still awake, and needing the loo. Thrusting her arms into the sleeves of her old Jaeger dressing-gown, she padded down the hall, aided by a light swathed in a green bag. How that brought back memories of her hospital years! She remembered presiding over a darkened ward at night, alert to any signs of distress from the thirty or so patients there, while dim lights here and there glowed softly, shrouded in their green coverings.

Back in her room, she crossed over to the window, which was now firmly closed. The bulk of the adjacent church loomed eerily close, partly illuminated by a streetlight shining into the alleyway. She squinted up to her right, where there was a partial view of the sky. The moon came out from behind a cloud, seeming to race across the sky before disappearing again.

Down below, something moved stealthily. Maudie tensed, straining her eyes to see more. The moon reappeared suddenly, and she caught a glimpse of a dark figure, apparently strewing something on the ground at the foot of the church wall. For a moment, she couldn't think what was happening, and then it dawned on her that she was seeing the arsonist at work!

Frantically ringing her bell, she waited impatiently for help to arrive.

'Mrs Bryant! What on earth is the matter? Do you want to wake the whole house?' This was a different nurse, bristling with indignation.

'I've got to call my husband!' Maudie gasped. 'Where's the nearest telephone?'

'Do you know what time it is? Three o'clock in the morning! Now, let me help you back into bed. Would you like some hot milk to help you get to sleep?'

'There's an arsonist outside, trying to set fire to the church!' Maudie hissed. 'I have to speak to my husband immediately!'

'It's all right, Mrs Bryant; I expect you've had a nightmare. Let's get you back to sleep now, and I expect you'll have a good laugh about this in the morning.'

'I haven't been to sleep at all yet, and you'll be laughing on the other side of your face if you don't let me call the police immediately! Don't you understand that if the church catches fire, The Elms will be in danger as well?'

The nurse still looked uncertain. Maudie took hold of the girl's sleeve and shook it. 'Listen to me, Nurse, very carefully. I am not having a nightmare. My husband is Detective Sergeant Dick Bryant who works out of Midvale. Surely you've heard there's been an arsonist on the loose, setting fire to churches all over the county. He's here now; I've just seen him. Unless you want all your mothers and babies burned to death in their beds, you'll let me sound the alarm now! Is that clear?'

29

'Come on! *Come on!* Where are you, Dick?' Maudie stood at the window in a fever of impatience. The night should have been filled with the sound of sirens, and the police should have been on the scene, wielding truncheons and blowing their whistles! Hadn't that fool of a nurse telephoned the station?

Her heart sank as she realized that the force was hardly likely to arrive in large numbers. Midvale simply didn't have the manpower, especially at night. Would they have called in reinforcements; and, if so, would they arrive in time?

She jumped at the touch of a hand on her sleeve. 'I've done what you wanted, Mrs Bryant,' the nurse whispered, 'but you must come back to bed now. If there's anything to worry about, which I very much doubt, I'm sure the police will soon have it under control.'

'Not blinking likely!' Maudie muttered.

'Don't you understand? There's an arsonist down there, and we're all in deadly danger! Shouldn't we wake the mothers and wrap up the babies, in case we have to evacuate the place?'

Rolling her eyes, Nurse Billings edged over to the window and peered out.

'Don't let him see you!' Maudie hissed.

The girl shrugged. 'I can't see a thing!'

But out in the street, something moved. Just a shadow, then another. It dawned on Maudie that the police wouldn't come roaring in as if they were actors in a Western movie. This was no *Gunfight at the O.K. Corral*! They would move in quietly, hoping to catch the arsonist in the act. She screwed up her eyes, trying to make out what was happening.

A flicker of flame showed against the dark wall of the church, wavered in the breeze and then died. Cautiously, Maudie opened the window an inch or two, and the pungent smell of petrol greeted her nostrils.

Hardly daring to breathe, she bent closer to the glass. Oh, why didn't someone come? 'Did you alert the fire brigade, Nurse?' she whispered.

'What? Oh, no, of course I didn't. You can get into trouble for phoning in false alarms, you know!'

Maudie wanted to shake the girl. Had she no imagination at all? She could only hope that the police had taken the situation more seriously and had the firemen standing by.

Moments later, everything happened at once. A torrent of flame shot up, illuminating the figure of the arsonist. Dressed in dark clothing, he appeared to be of medium height, but beyond that there was no clue as to his identity as his features were hidden by a balaclava helmet. Two men burst out of the shadows then; at least, she supposed they were men, for even in the light of the leaping flames it was impossible to see who they were.

Screams ripped through the night-time quiet. As the two women watched in horror, the figure of the arsonist became engulfed in fire. For one wild moment before realization set in, Maudie was reminded of the effigies of Guy Fawkes that children burned on Bonfire Night. However wrong-headed the arsonist might be, this was still a human being, about to meet a horrible death.

Beside her, Nurse Billings gave a low cry, averting her gaze. Unable to look away, Maudie saw one of the newcomers tearing off his overcoat as he advanced on the stricken man, rolling him in its folds as he bore him to the ground. She bit back a cry as she recognized the stocky outline of that heroic newcomer as her beloved husband, Dick Bryant.

Please let Dick not be burned! Please let them be all right! As she screamed her silent prayer, she felt a gush of moisture where she stood, and she groaned aloud. What a time for the membranes to rupture!

'What's wrong, Mrs Bryant? Not having pains, are you?' Alerted by Maudie's little gasp, Nurse Billings remembered where she was. Wordlessly, Maudie pointed to the little puddle on the floor.

'Oh, your waters have broken, Mrs Bryant. Nothing to worry about. It just means that Baby is on its way. The sac of fluid in which he or she has been enclosed for the past nine months has now burst, you see.'

'Charming!' Maudie said dryly.

'And you must come away from the window now, and lie down while I take your vital signs. We mustn't get over-excited, must we? I expect we'll go into labour quite soon now.'

'You may be going into labour, Nurse, but I can assure you that I'm not. And I refuse to go anywhere until I make sure that everything is all right down below,' Maudie snapped.

The clanging of bells heralded the arrival of the fire brigade and an ambulance. Light from their headlamps illuminated the scene, and Maudie was relieved to see Dick scrambling to his feet to make way for the ambulance attendants. The crumpled figure on the ground was loaded onto a stretcher, and she was glad to see an oxygen mask being placed over his face. He wasn't dead, then.

Dick glanced up at the window and raised a hand in salute. He could hardly have made out the two women standing there, but he did know his Maudie. Heavily pregnant as she was, she was in no condition to have taken part in the action, but by hook or by crook she'd manage to insinuate herself into the picture somehow! He turned away then and clambered into the back of the ambulance, which then sped off. She hoped he was simply going along to accompany the suspect and was not actually in need of treatment himself.

*   *   *

Dick sat at Maudie's bedside, enjoying an early-morning cup of tea. Knowing that she would be worried about his possible role in the affair, he wanted to reassure her, but he had experienced some difficulty in managing to get past the day sister at the nursing home.

'I'm afraid you cannot see your wife now, Mr Bryant! You will have to return during visiting hours. We cannot have husbands cluttering up the place in the morning when the staff have their work to do!' She looked down at his bandaged hands. 'And what on earth have you been up to? I hope you don't have some sort of nasty rash there!'

A reporter from the *Midvale Chronicle* had crept in on soft-soled suede shoes, and was waiting behind the admissions desk, taking in every word. He spoke up now, employing typical journalese to get his point across.

'If it wasn't for the detective sergeant here, you might not have a nursing home to get cluttered up, Nurse!'

She glared at him. 'What on earth are you babbling about? And it's Sister to you, if you don't mind!'

'Sister, then. Well, the arsonist struck again last night, in an attempt to burn down the church next door. If the fire had taken hold before the fire brigade arrived, your little kingdom could have gone up in smoke as well. And we all know that it's the smoke that actually kills, before the flames ever reach the victims.'

Sister looked sceptical. Dick shuffled his feet.

'DS Bryant is the hero of the hour,' the

reporter went on. 'The arsonist somehow managed to set fire to himself, and it was the sergeant here who threw him down and managed to beat out the flames, thereby saving the chap's life. And I'm willing to bet that the nasty rash, as you call it, is at best some very nasty blisters.'

'And what is more,' Dick said, seizing his chance when he managed to get a word in at last, 'I'm pretty sure it was my wife who caught a glimpse of the arsonist from her window, which I happen to know overlooks the church, and sounded the alarm. Or at least prevailed upon one of your staff to give us a ring. I don't know how much she saw, but if she realized it was me tackling the chap, she must be worried indeed. And that certainly won't do her blood pressure any good. So, if you'd let me have a few minutes with her, please, I'd be very grateful.'

'Well, I suppose it wouldn't hurt, under the circumstances,' Sister admitted. 'And I daresay you won't say no to a cup of tea?'

Maudie's eyes lit up when she saw

Dick. 'I've been worried sick about you! Are you all right? What happened to your hands? What about the arsonist? Who is he? Is he alive?'

'Whoa, steady on, old girl!' Dick said, laughing. 'No lasting damage to either of us, the doc says. I can't say the same for my new mac, though! The chap's clothes were on fire and I had to use my raincoat to snuff out the flames.'

'Have you had a chance to interview him yet? Any idea why he's been doing this?'

'Actually, he's made a full confession. When the boss asked him why he'd done it, and why pick on churches in particular, he said he'd done it to punish God.'

'Oh?'

'Apparently, his mother was killed during the Blitz when her home in London collapsed on top of her. According to him, she was a very religious woman, a regular church attendee who spent her days doing good deeds in the community. She brought up her children to trust in God, so when she was killed her son was greatly disillusioned and wanted to pay God back.'

'And by burning down churches he felt he was hurting Him by destroying His houses, I suppose.'

'It wasn't just that. This chap wanted to show other believers that their faith is misplaced. 'If the Lord is all-powerful, why didn't he save our chapel?' That sort of thing.'

'Poor tortured man,' Maudie said. 'At least it wasn't teenagers doing it for kicks. Who is he, anyway? I know he attacked churches in several different places, but where is he actually from?'

'Right here in Midvale. He happens to be someone you know, Maudie!'

'What? Who?'

'John Landry.'

'You mean the RSPCA man!'

'The RSPCA have been quick to disclaim any connection with him. That is to say, he has no official standing with them. He's simply one of the local volunteers who help out by going round with the collecting tin on flag day.'

'Good grief! And I suppose that was a

good cover story when he went about looking for suitable venues for his bonfires! What will happen to him, Dick?'

'Oh, he'll be remanded for psychiatric assessment, I should think. After that, it's up to the courts.'

Maudie shuddered. 'I imagine that's what he was up to that day in our church; deciding how to go about his next move. There are centuries-old wooden beams up there in the belfry. Perhaps he thought that was a good place to start a fire. He couldn't very well have done the job outside; the thick stone walls would have prevented that.'

'Mrs Blunt had the right idea when she said they should keep the church locked up when there were no services scheduled,' Dick remembered.

'I know, but the vicar didn't agree with that. He said that God's house is open to all, and to prevent access to it would be contrary to the church's purpose.'

'Oh, well, it's all over now; just so long as we've got the right man, and we don't have any copycat crimes,' Dick said. 'I say, is that a box of chocolates you've got there? You haven't had visitors bearing gifts, have you?'

'If you must know, I brought it in with me. Just as well. I need something to sustain me while I'm stuck in here with nothing to do but wait for the next meal to arrive.'

'What about me? This expectant father business is wearing me down. I feel a bit hollow in the pit of the stomach.'

'You can have one chocolate-covered brazil nut, and no more!' Maudie told him, handing him the box. With a devilish smile, he took two.

30

'It's a boy!' Maudie heard the words through a haze of pain and wooziness. Harsh lights overhead beamed down on her, forcing her to close her eyes against the glare. She waited. Seconds later, a reedy little wail filled the room.

'No need to slap this one's bottom!' the midwife exclaimed with satisfaction. 'Meet your son, Mrs Bryant!' As she draped the baby over her patient's tummy, Maudie reached down to caress the damp little head.

That's a funny way to put it, she thought drowsily. We've already been together for nine months, and for the last four and a half I've felt every squirm and kick. This one is destined to be a football player, I'm sure! 'Hello, Rover!' she said aloud. 'Welcome to the world!'

'Rover!' the midwife exclaimed. 'What sort of name is that for a bonny wee man?'

Maudie wanted to explain that in the early days of her pregnancy, having no way of knowing the gender of the baby, she and Dick had loving referred to their child as Rover, but since then they'd acquired a dog who had inherited the name. 'Can't call him that now,' she managed.

'No, indeed you can't, Mrs Bryant. You must choose a good, solid name; like Angus, say, or Maximilian, if this one is to grow up to conquer the world!'

* * *

Outside in the waiting room, Dick had been pacing up and down in time-honoured style. Muffled sounds had come to his ears now and then; deep groans, and once a scream. What were they doing to her in there? It sounded to him like a torture chamber. It was all he could do to stop himself bursting in to see what was going on. Why was it taking so long? Fourteen seemingly endless hours had passed since someone had tele-phoned to let him know that his wife had gone into labour.

What if anything had happened to his Maudie? he asked himself miserably. He couldn't bear to lose her now. She had laughed at his fears early on, saying that women didn't die in childbirth nowadays, which did little to reassure him. He knew that medical science had come a long way since his great-aunt had died struggling to deliver her thirteenth child; but, even so, childbirth was never quite without risk, was it? Maudie was well up in years to be having a first baby. Couldn't that mean that the odds of survival were against her?

He believed that Maudie was a magnificent midwife, and she certainly had an enviable success rate while practising her craft. But somebody else had to help her now. Who was this woman? Was she properly qualified? Would she know enough to summon Dr Dean if something went wrong?

The door opened, and the woman he'd maligned peered around it. 'Hello, Daddy! It's a boy!'

Confused, he frowned at her. 'Are you sure?'

She laughed. 'I've been in this business for a good many years, mister, and I'm never wrong! You have a son.'

'Is my wife all right? Can I see them?'

'In a little while, Mr Bryant. We have a bit of tidying up to do in here first. Go and sit down, do. You look as white as a sheet.' She disappeared inside, but not before a frantic wailing reached his ears. It was his own child making all that noise! They had a baby! He had a son! He collapsed into a waiting armchair, overcome with emotion. Dick Bryant was a father!

* * *

After a while, a nurse emerged from the delivery room, pushing a cot on wheels. When she paused beside Dick to let him see the baby, he saw a red-faced infant swaddled in a blue blanket, with one miniature hand struggling to get free.

'Isn't he rather small?' he wondered. 'Is he all right, Nurse?'

'Small!' she said indignantly. 'He

weighs seven pounds six ounces! There's not a thing wrong with this baby!'

'But his head looks a bit — um — squashed to me!'

'Your head would look a bit squashed too, if you'd just been pushed down a tunnel that's too tight a fit!' the nurse declared. 'This child will look perfectly normal a few hours from now.'

'Well, if you say so,' Dick said doubtfully.

'I do say so! Now, if you'll stand aside, please, I want to take this baby to the nursery. Lying out here in the draught is not good for him,'

'But can't I just . . .'

'No, you cannot. Your wife will be out in a minute, and then she'll want you to tell her what a clever girl she is. Do you think you can do that?'

'Er, yes, I suppose so.' Suddenly all Dick's fears fell away, and he was overcome with the glory of it all. They were parents! They had a little boy! All was right with the world.

★ ★ ★

Maudie was propped up in bed with what looked like a mountain of hot buttered toast in front of her. 'Oh, no you don't!' she scolded, smacking Dick's hand as he reached out to take a slice. 'I need every scrap of this after what I've just been through. Think yourself lucky they've given you a cup of tea. All you've had to do is pace up and down for a bit.'

'It felt like months,' he told her. 'Was it very bad, old girl?'

'It's over now,' she assured him. Overcome with the euphoria that comes with giving birth successfully, Maudie didn't want to dwell on her ordeal. 'The next thing we have to think about is his name. Somehow none of the ones we've come up with seem right, now he's actually here.'

'I've been thinking,' Dick said slowly. 'Would you mind if we called him Charles, after my father? It can be his second name if you don't care for it very much.'

'Charles Bryant,' Maudie agreed, her heart going out to the father that Dick had barely known. Charlie Bryant had died in the mud of Flanders when his son had just started school, and his widow had remained faithful to his memory for the rest of her life. 'And Richard for a second name,' she went on.

'Charles Richard Bryant,' Dick said, trying it on for size. 'I like it. Sounds like a future prime minister, doesn't it?'

'Or a Harley Street specialist, or a bishop, or a world-famous author,' Maudie said, laughing.

'Just as long as it's not a con man or a bigamist, that's all that matters.'

'Oh, you! What a thing to say! We'll have to bring him up very carefully so there's no chance of any such thing!'

As a policeman Dick was well aware that many a villain was the product of a decent home, where parents had striven to show their children a good example. Why some people turned out badly despite having had a good background was a mystery, just as it was nothing short of a miracle that some people achieved great things despite having had all the cards stacked against them from birth. He and Maudie could only do their best for little Charlie, in the hope that he would grow up to have a happy, successful and productive life.

* * *

'How are you feeling, Nurse?' Mrs Blunt asked, when she dropped in to visit Maudie later that afternoon. 'I expect you're glad it's all over.'

'I've had a good sleep, and they've let me have little Charlie with me for a while, so I feel fit for anything. Mind you, I'm not one of those women you read about occasionally, who are out of bed scrubbing the kitchen floor within hours of giving birth!'

'Surely that's a myth,' Joan Blunt protested, 'I mean, why would anyone want to? Now, I've got a few things for you here. Mrs Grant has sent this posy from her garden; she says she's sorry she doesn't have any blue flowers except lobelia, and that doesn't sit very well in a vase. Blue for a boy, you know? Still, these snapdragons look cheerful, don't they? And this is from Cora Beasley.' She handed over a small wicker basket containing a variety of hand lotions, talcum powder and scented soap.

'How kind,' Maudie murmured, giving an appreciative sniff at a tablet of Royal Rose.

'And, knowing you, I stopped at Bentham's on the way here and brought you these!'

Joan Blunt lifted the lid of a bakery box to reveal three chocolate eclairs, oozing with cream.

'Just what I wanted!' Maudie enthused. 'I'll be the fattest new mum on the planet, but right now I don't care!' She drew her finger along the lid of the box where some cream had worked its way out of one of the pastries, and licked it with a sigh of bliss.

'Now, do tell me what's been happening in Llandyfan,' she said. 'It seems an age since I was there.'

'Well, of course the main thing is that the arsonist has been caught. Or perhaps that's not the right term for it under the circumstances. I've heard that he turned himself in. Is that right?'

'That's what Dick says.'

'You can't imagine the change in my poor husband. He's hardly slept for weeks, ever since this arson business started, terrified that St John's would go up in smoke unless he could do something to prevent it. And I thought he'd have a heart attack when he heard that John Landry was responsible! He's quite sure that if the man hadn't been seen coming down from the belfry that day, he'd have returned some night to finish the job.'

'Well, he can relax now. How is Rover getting along with Perkin, by the way? It's so good of you to put him up while I'm in here.'

'My dear, it's the strangest thing! I came downstairs this morning, and what do you think I found?'

'Not the mangled remains of the vicar's breakfast sausages, I hope!'

'No! Your dog curled up on the hearthrug with Perkin snoring away between his paws! The cat must have escaped from the spare room and come down in the night, and they somehow managed to make friends with each other.'

'Good grief! I never would have thought it possible. Of course, we don't know a thing about Rover's past life; he could well have come from a home where there were cats. It may be that when he's chased after Perkin in the past it wasn't with malicious intent, but only because he wanted to play.'

'Whatever the reason, they're firm friends now.'

United in the urge to steal food, Maudie thought. She'd have to keep an eye on those two, or they'd be creating mayhem while she was busy with the baby.

31

Little Charlie was only three days old when Maudie began to feel restless. Life was comfortable at The Elms, and the staff were all very kind, but she longed to be at home in her own surroundings. There was much to be said for being able to make yourself a cup of tea on the spur of the moment, or to take an old favourite down from your bookshelf as the urge dictated.

She considered discharging herself from the nursing home — she wasn't ill, after all — but prudence dictated that she should stay put. The good thing about The Elms was that they kept the babies in the nursery rather than at their mothers' bedsides, only bringing them in at feeding time. When Charlie had finished his two o'clock feed, she was glad enough to hand him to a nurse so she could sink back into sleep. If he continued to bawl, it would be someone else's job to comfort him. Was she an unnatural mother? Common sense told her that she was lucky to have this nine days' respite instead of walking the floor all night with a crying baby. The pair of them would go home soon enough, and then she'd wish she was back at The Elms!

Dick arrived one evening carrying a bunch of grapes and a selection of women's magazines. Maudie pounced on them with delight. 'Just what I needed!' she exclaimed. 'They have magazines here for patients to borrow, but they're all old and tattered. Some of them go back to before the war! And if I see one more wartime recipe for meatless shepherd's pie, I shall scream!'

Dick helped himself to a grape. 'Better be careful with these,' he warned her, chewing carefully. 'They've got pips in.'

'Surely you don't believe that old myth that swallowing pips can cause appendicitis?' Maudie said, laughing.

'Not exactly, but they could do you a mischief if one goes down the wrong way.' He swallowed and reached for two more, which he popped into his mouth.

'How was work today?' Maudie asked.

'Very interesting, actually. We seem to have got a lead on what Basil Fleming did with the money he stole.'

'No, really?'

'A letter came in the post, addressed to 'The detectives in the Fleming murder case'. It was a long, rambling screed from a man in Leicestershire who had been on holiday to Bath, a coach outing with his church choir. They'd stopped at some small town on the way for a lunch and comfort break, when he happened to spot an estate agency.'

Maudie yawned. 'And?'

'The name over the door proclaimed it to be the Basil Raymond Agency. He — the choir man — thought we might want to investigate that.'

'What's supposed to be so funny about that, then?'

'I couldn't see it either, but we have to follow up any lead we can get, so I put in a call to this chap's local police station, and asked them to send a constable round to see if he could find out more. I heard back just before I left to come here, and lo and behold! This Thomas Williams happens to be one of Fleming's victims. Old-age pensions don't go very far these days, and he was afraid he wouldn't be able to manage after he retired, so he handed his life savings over to Fleming to be invested. The certificate he was given in return isn't worth the paper it was written on, but it is signed with his name in full: Basil Raymond Fleming.'

'Oh, I see! So this chap thought that Fleming may have sunk the money into a business using part of his own name. I suppose it's possible, but Raymond is a common enough surname. This is probably just coincidence, don't you think?'

'Maybe; maybe not. We shall have to see. Now then, how is my son and heir?'

'Thriving, I'm glad to say. I can't wait to get home, though. Have you seen Rover? Is he missing me?'

'He was certainly glad to see me when I went over last night to take him for a run, but he didn't mention your name at all.'

'Fool! And stop scoffing down those grapes, or there won't be any left for me.'

'So who said anything about them being for you?' Dick countered.

⋆　⋆　⋆

Lillian Grant arrived during visiting hours, carrying a large bouquet of summer flowers. 'I asked that receptionist girl for a vase, and she looked down her nose at these and told me I shouldn't have brought so many! 'What do you mean by that?' I asked, and do you know what she said, Mrs Bryant?'

Maudie smiled and shook her head.

'It makes work for the nurses, she said, and that's not what they're here for. They have to take all the flowers out of the rooms at night and bring them back in the next morning! Did you ever hear such a load of codswallop?'

Maudie knew this was common practice, but didn't feel up to explaining the reasoning behind it. Now she came to think about it, 'codswallop' just about described it. If flowers gave off noxious vapours at night, then why did people leave their bedroom windows open in summer to let all the night-time scents pour in?

'The flowers are lovely! Thank you very much! Do sit down, Mrs Grant, and tell me all your news.'

'Not much to tell, really. Our Godfrey is on his way back to Canada now. We've had such a lovely time together, and we can't thank your hubby enough for helping us to find each other again after all these years!'

'I suppose you'll be off to Canada next!'

Lillian shuddered. 'Not me! You won't catch me going up in one of those flying machines, and I don't fancy going by boat either, not after what happened to that *Titanic*! No, we'll keep in touch by post, and one of these days I may get a telephone put in so we can have a chat at Christmas.'

'Travel isn't for everybody,' Maudie said.

'No, indeed, but I tell you this, Mrs Bryant! If they still allowed public hanging I'd travel to the far side of the moon to watch that evil Fleming swing!

Our poor Fred didn't deserve to die, and you and I had a narrow escape, too, remember!'

'I certainly remember you trying to brain him with that warming pan!' Maudie said. 'And very grateful I was, too!'

Lillian blushed. 'I don't know how I found the nerve! I'd never hurt a fly in the normal way of things. But when I saw him trying to throttle you, I came over all queer. It was like I was getting back at him for what he did to Fred. It's a mercy I didn't kill the brute, or I'd be in a prison cell by now, waiting to meet the hangman.'

'Oh, I don't think it would have come to that,' Maudie murmured, and the conversation turned to other things. She longed to pass on the latest developments in the case against Basil Fleming, but Dick had given her the news in confidence and she knew that careless talk could affect the case against the killer, not to mention landing Dick in trouble at work.

* * *

The great day arrived at last. Maudie stepped carefully out of The Elms, carrying baby Charlie wrapped in a blue blanket. Dick followed behind, weighed down by a small suitcase, three damp bunches of flowers wrapped in newspaper, and three carrier bags containing gifts that had been delivered for mother and baby.

Charlie slept peacefully in his Moses basket during the twelve-mile journey home in the car, and neither did he stir when he was lovingly placed in the treasure cot in his very own bedroom. Maudie and Dick stood hand in hand, looking down at his dear little face, while tears slowly dripped over Maudie's cheeks.

'Buck up, old girl,' Dick whispered. 'Worse things happen at sea!'

'It's just that I'm so happy!' she sniffed, dabbing at her eyes with a damp hankie. 'All these years of bringing babies into the world, and I never thought I'd see the day when I had one of my own!' Silently, they tiptoed out of the room, not wishing to disturb the sleeping infant. He would begin to assert his presence in the household soon enough!

Their next task was to bring Rover home. Maudie stood outside to welcome him, afraid that his joyous yelping would awaken Charlie. Later, when she was seated in her favourite armchair with the baby on her lap, it was time to introduce him to the new member of the family.

With Dick holding his collar, 'just in case', the dog advanced on Maudie, sniffing cautiously. He took a step backwards when the baby emitted a tiny warble, but then, gazing up at Maudie with a puzzled expression, he advanced again. His tail began to wag slowly and then he sank down at Maudie's feet with a heavy sigh.

'Well, so that's all right, then,' Dick said. 'That dog has come a long way since he first arrived. He's made friends with that cat and now he seems to approve of the baby! We'll have to keep a sharp eye on him at first, of course.'

'And I'll have to keep the larder window firmly closed,' Maudie remarked. 'We can't risk Perkin coming near the

That will be for the courts to decide, I suppose, and it will take the wisdom of Solomon to sort that out. I'm just thankful that my job doesn't extend that far.'

* * *

One Sunday morning in autumn, the Bryants stood at the baptismal font in St John's Church while the congregation looked on in admiration. Many of the children who were present that day had been ushered into the world by Maudie, and now here she was with her own baby.

The godparents were the vicar's wife, Joan Blunt, and Dick's friend, Constable Bill Brewer. Both had been the attendants at Maudie and Dick's wedding. But none of the watchers were interested in those upright persons, because all eyes were on the baby.

Charles Richard Bryant was dressed in a lacy christening robe that had been knitted for him by his mother. The pattern had almost driven her mad, and the fact that the wool was three-ply and

baby. It's not that I believe those old wives' tales about cats deliberately smothering babies, but all the same, it wouldn't do to have him jumping in the cradle!'

As the weeks passed, Maudie realized how fortunate she'd been to have had nurses to look after Charlie while she lolled in bed, getting her strength back. Now it seemed as if she had only just dropped off to sleep at night when he woke up, noisily demanding sustenance. And as if that wasn't enough, Rover joined in the act with shrill yaps, adding to the cacophony while he scratched at their bedroom door to alert them to the baby's need.

Dick became used to stumbling downstairs, bleary-eyed, on his way to work. 'I think I'm too old for this fatherhood business,' he groaned to Maudie, when she was preparing his breakfast after a particularly wakeful night. Charlie had woken up on cue, but been too sleepy to suckle, and Maudie had had trouble keeping him awake. Once back in his cot, however, he had soon got up steam and the whole process had to be gone through again. 'We should have done this years ago, and the boy would be grown up by now!'

'Possibly presenting us with a whole new set of problems,' Maudie said. She wasn't usually so downbeat, but this sleep deprivation was getting to her. If she were twenty years younger, she might be better equipped to cope!

As the weeks went by, and spring gave way to summer, little Charlie Bryant became easier to live with. He began sleeping through the night, and it was a red-letter day when he recognized his mother's face and responded with a toothless smile.

Things went well with Dick's work, too, and it was with great pride that he was able to report progress on the Fleming case; firstly to his boss, DI Goodman, and then to Maudie.

'Basil Raymond Enterprises is indeed Fleming's baby,' he told her. 'He's had quite an operation going. All the money he stole has gone into building houses, which of course are desperately needed since the war. No doubt they've sold like hot cakes.'

'How public-spirited of him!' Maudie sneered. 'And I suppose in his Fleming persona he's been able to arrange mortgages for people through the bank!'

'I doubt if that's the case. Our investigation is ongoing, of course, but so far we haven't found any buyers from the Midvale district. After all, his housing estates are nowhere near here, and I expect that getting himself transferred to this area was to distance himself from all that. As far as anyone knew, he was an upright citizen, working his way up in the hierarchy of the bank. He might have gone on in the same way forever, had it not been for Fred Woolton recognizing him from out of the past. A bit of bad luck, that was,' Dick concluded.

'Even worse luck for poor Fred,' Maudie said. 'What will happen now? Will any of the investors get their money back, do you think?'

'That remains to be seen. If most of the money has gone into building houses, which people have bought in good faith, I don't know how it could be freed up to recompense the people Fleming conned.

the needles were small hadn't helped. Maudie had several times come close to abandoning the project, but she had persevered and won through. The finished product was not as fine as the antique robe worn by little Princess Anne a year earlier, and her brother Charles before her, but it was just as valuable in terms of the love and care invested in it.

Maudie looked around her. She felt like the richest woman in the world, standing beside the man she loved with all her heart, holding their own precious child. The ancient church was filled with friends and neighbours, all of whom would play some part in little Charlie's life. Together with Dick and the godparents she renounced the devil and all his works on behalf of her tiny innocent son.

As they joined in a rousing hymn, Maudie gave thanks that after all that had happened recently, they had indeed triumphed over the work of the devil. Once again she had been saved from an untimely death at the hands of someone who meant to kill her, and although Fred Woolton hadn't been so fortunate, his killer had been caught. Lillian Grant had been reunited with her long-lost brother, Godfrey. The arsonist was behind bars, and The Reverend Harold Blunt's beloved church was safe.

The Bryants stepped out in the sunshine. A small child darted up to Maudie, tugging insistently at her skirt. 'My granny says ladies find their babies in the cabbage patch, but you haven't got one, 'cos I looked. So, where did you get Charlie?'

Maudie looked down at the child. 'The angels brought him, dear. You know how Father Christmas brings you presents? Well, angels bring babies, you see.'

The little girl frowned. 'Did you send them a note up the chimney, then, asking them to bring you a baby?'

'Something like that,' Maudie said, smiling. Then, with her husband at her side and their baby in her arms, she walked forward into the future.